THE EDGE
OF THE
EMPIRE

TALES OF ROME

THE EDGE
OF THE
EMPIRE

KATHY LEE

Copyright © Kathy Lee 2006
First published 2005
ISBN 1 84427 167 6

Scripture Union, 207–209 Queensway, Bletchley, Milton Keynes, MK2 2EB, England.
Email: info@scriptureunion.org.uk
Website: www.scriptureunion.org.uk

Scripture Union Australia
Locked Bag 2, Central Coast Business Centre, NSW 2252
Website: www.scriptureunion.org.au

Scripture Union USA
PO Box 987, Valley Forge, PA 19482
Website: www.scriptureunion.org

The right of Kathy Lee to be identified as author of this work has been asserted by her in accordance with the Copyright, Designs and Patents Act 1988.

British Library Cataloguing-in-Publication Data.
A catalogue record of this book is available from the British Library.

Printed and bound in Great Britain by Creative Print and Design (Wales), Ebbw Vale.

Internal illustration by Christopher Rothero.
Cover design by GoBallistic.
Internal design and layout by Author and Publisher Services.

 Scripture Union is an international Christian charity working with churches in more than 130 countries, providing resources to bring the good news about Jesus Christ to children, young people and families and to encourage them to develop spiritually through the Bible and prayer.

As well as our network of volunteers, staff and associates who run holidays, church-based events and school Christian groups, we produce a wide range of publications and support those who use our resources through training programmes.

Other books by the same author

A Captive in Rome
Rome in Flames

Fabulous Phoebe
Phoebe's Fortune
Phoebe finds her feet
Phoebe's book of Body Image, Boys and Bible bits

Seasiders: Runners
Seasiders: Liar
Seasiders: Joker
Seasiders: Winner
Seasiders: Angels

Flood Alert

CONTENTS

I

THE BRITISH OCEAN

"Pirates?" asked Felix. "Are you serious?"

"Oh, yes," said the merchant. "There are pirates sailing the British Ocean, all right. The Roman navy does what it can to control them. But you can't expect the navy to patrol the entire coast of Britain and Gaul."

Felix looked around the harbour as if he expected – or even hoped – to see pirates appear at any moment. The merchant smiled.

"Not here," he said. "Out on the open sea – that's where you're likely to meet them."

"Have you ever met any?" Felix asked.

"Don't be stupid. If I had, I wouldn't be here talking to you now."

We were in a busy port on the northern coast of Gaul. Felix and I were waiting on the quayside, while our friend Tiro talked to the captain of a ship which might take us to Britain.

Britain! I hadn't seen it for four years. I could hardly believe that in a few more days, I might be back in the land of my birth.

I looked at the ship that we might be sailing in, if Tiro could agree a price. It was built of oak, with a single mast and two steering oars. The large sail, rolled up at the moment, was made of brown leather. There was a high, curved prow and stern.

The last time I sailed in a ship like that, I was 11 years old. It was in the year of the great rebellion. My father had been killed in the final battle, when the Romans defeated Queen Boudicca's army. My brother Conan and I were captured, taken to Rome and sold as slaves.

When Conan was freed, he set out to find his way home. I had no way of knowing if he had succeeded, or if my mother and sisters were still alive. During the years in Rome, I thought about them often. One day, I promised myself... one day...

And now the day had almost come.

***

Our journey had actually begun in Rome, the previous year. That summer there was a great fire which destroyed half the city. The emperor, Nero, put the blame on Christians for starting the fire. Many believers were arrested and killed.

I had become a believer, thanks to Tiro. He was an African who had spent 15 years – most of his adult life – in Rome as a slave. Through him I got to know a small group of Christians who met together in secret. Felix, a free-born Roman, was one of them. He was 16, a year older than me.

The three of us had been arrested, but we'd managed to escape and flee from Rome, along with some of our friends. We had spent the winter months in central Gaul, far enough from Rome to feel safe. Our friends were still there, finding work to do, making new lives for themselves.

But as spring came on, I began to feel restless. I was so much nearer to my homeland now. Why shouldn't I try to find my way back to my own village? If it still existed... if the Romans hadn't destroyed it.

When I started talking about the trip, Felix was full of enthusiasm. He loved the thought of travel and adventure.

"I'll come with you, Bryn," he offered.

"Would you really?"

"Just for a visit, I mean," he said, hastily. "I don't think I'd want to stay there. But we'd need quite a lot of money. Hey, maybe we could actually make some money out of the trip. Buy things, bring them back, sell them – people do that all the time. I bet Tiro would come too, if we asked him."

Suddenly the whole idea began to seem more solid, more than just a daydream.

"Your mother won't want you to go," I said. His mother was an anxious kind of person. She would hate the thought of her only son travelling to the edge of the empire and back.

"She keeps nagging me to find a proper job," he said. "Trading is a job, isn't it?"

Somehow he managed to persuade his mother that the trip would be perfectly safe. After all, the south of Britain had been in Roman hands for over twenty years. Surely it must be quite civilised by now...

Septimus, one of our friends, was a wealthy trader. He loaned us some money for the trip, because he wanted to know more about Britain.

"Write everything down," he said to Felix, the only one of us who could write. "Keep your eyes open in towns and marketplaces. I suppose they do have marketplaces in Britain? Tell me all about it when you return."

He knew, of course, that I might not return from the trip, if I managed to find my family. But if I failed in that, there would be little to keep me in Britain. I wished I could see into the future. Where would I be a month from now?

Then I told myself there was no point in worrying. Only God could see what the future might hold for me. Wherever I ended up, in Gaul or Britain or even Rome, my life was in his hands.

***

The ship was full of activity. The sailors were hoisting heavy clay wine-jars on board, using a pulley system attached to the mast, and lowering them into the hold.

Slaves carried wooden crates up the gangplank. The middle-aged merchant – I guessed he was a Gaulish Celt, although he spoke to us in Latin – kept a watchful eye on them.

"Is all this wine going to Britain?" Felix asked him.

"Yes. I hear the British tribes have developed quite a thirst for it. In Britain, an amphora of Falernian is worth as much as a slave! When I've sold my wine, I'll buy slaves and ship them back over here. I should make a good profit." He rubbed his hands, as if he could already feel the money coming in.

I hated the thought of my own people being sold into exile. "Do you *have* to buy slaves?" I asked him. "Can't you trade in other things, instead of human lives?"

He looked at me as if I was crazy. "I don't see what's wrong with trading in slaves. Some of them will have quite a good life, if they're prepared to work. But what takes the two of you to Britain?"

"Actually, we are traders too," Felix said, grandly. "We may import wool – British wool fetches a good price in Rome. Or tin, or possibly jewellery."

The man laughed. "How old are you, son?"

Felix drew himself up to his full height – not equal to mine, although he was older than me. (My people, the Celts, are generally taller and fairer than the Romans.)

Looking as haughty as an emperor on a coin, Felix said, "I'm 16, and a Roman citizen."

"Are you, indeed? You may not find that helps you much in Britain. It's a pretty uncivilised place, I hear. Full of barbarian tribes, ready to rebel at the slightest excuse. Many of them hate the name of Rome. I don't suppose you speak the Celtic language, do you? How do you intend to trade?"

"I'll let Bryn do the talking."

The merchant stared at me, then back at Felix. "Young fools. You'll be robbed and cheated, and end up begging the money for your passage back here."

"Anyone who tries to rob us will have Tiro to reckon with," I said, just as Tiro himself came striding along the quayside. He looked like what he used to be: a warrior, tough and strong. Strangers were often wary of him, until they got to know his calm, peaceable nature.

"Well?" said Felix eagerly. "Will the ship take us?"

"It's all settled," Tiro said. "If the winds are right, we sail tomorrow."

II

BREAKING WAVES

Early next morning, as the ship left the shelter of the river mouth, I saw Felix was looking rather anxious. Unlike me, he'd never sailed before.

"When do we start feeling seasick?" he muttered.

"What? You won't feel seasick on a day like this. The sea's as calm as a pond."

"I never saw a pond with waves like those," he said.

"That's nothing at all. I've been through much worse than that. You should see what the waves can do in the western ocean."

"Oh, stop boasting," said Felix. "You'll end up sounding like Costicos."

Costicos was the name of the merchant we'd met the day before. As we had waited for the ship to cast off, he'd told us about the voyages he'd undertaken, and the dangers of the seas. Someone he knew – or rather, the friend of a cousin of someone he knew – had actually sailed right round the northern tip of Britain. He'd seen whirlpools, ferocious storms, monstrous fishes, and creatures which were half-man, half-seal. I didn't believe much of this, but Felix listened, enthralled.

There was a stiff breeze blowing from the south-east. Instead of trying to go many miles east, to where the crossing would be narrower, the captain had decided to head straight out to sea. If the wind held, we should see Britain by nightfall.

I leant on the rail. The wind ruffled my hair, which hadn't been cut since I started thinking about this trip. Now my hair was too long by Roman standards, but too short for a man of the Iceni tribe. It was neither one thing nor another.

When I was taken away from my home, I was only 11. I'd changed a lot in the last four years. If I did manage to find my family, would they know me? Would I be able to recognise them? They might have changed too...

Perhaps this trip was a bad idea. I should have gone on daydreaming, and never tried to turn my dream into reality.

But it was too late. I couldn't turn back now.

***

As the morning passed, the coast of Gaul slowly dwindled behind us, until it vanished altogether. We were at the centre of a vast circle of sea and sky.

Nothing moved except the endless waves, and a few seagulls drifting on the wind.

"How much longer?" Felix asked one of the sailors.

"We must be almost halfway over," the sailor told him. The sailors, like Costicos, were mostly Celts from Gaul. Among themselves they spoke the Celtic language, but they changed easily into Latin if they needed to. Their land had been conquered by the Romans a long time ago, in the time of their great-grandfathers.

I asked the sailor if he'd been to Britain before.

"Many times," he said.

"What do you think of it?" asked Felix.

"Oh, I suppose it will be all right in a few more years, when it's civilised. At the moment you can't get a decent meal or a drink. And the weather! It always seems to be raining!"

"It's fine at the moment," I said, looking up at the sun.

"Yes, well, we're not in Britain yet."

The afternoon wore on. Still there was no sight of land ahead, and the wind was dropping. A misty haze rose out of the sea. The horizon disappeared; there was only a greyish blur where the sky seemed to merge with the water. Even the sun was dimmed, until it looked pale and flat, like an old, worn, silver coin.

The captain didn't look too worried while he still had the sun to guide him. But then the mist thickened. Our world shrank to a small patch of sea, ringed by fog. And now the sun was invisible.

The captain frowned. He had to try to steer using only the light winds and the waves – and either of them could change.

We sailed on and on. Surely by now land would be in sight, I thought, if it wasn't for this terrible fog. The captain told a sailor to climb the mast, in case anything could be seen from higher up.

"Where are we?" Costicos demanded. "Are we lost, Captain?"

The captain didn't answer him. Still we went on, hoping and praying that the fog would lift. After what seemed like hours – there was no way of knowing – the captain sent another sailor to the prow of the ship. He carried a long, thin rope with a lead weight tied to the end.

"What are you doing?" Felix asked him.

"Testing the depth of the water."

"Why?"

"Because we don't want to run aground, you idiot," he said.

The sailor swung the weight round and round like a stone in a sling, then let go of it. The weight fell into the water with a splash. Holding the rope's end, the sailor would be able to feel if the weight touched the sea bottom.

I stared down at the sea. It looked harmless enough; smooth, grey, whale-backed waves lifted us silently and slid away into the mist. But if we ran onto rocks, those same waves would pound against the ship, smashing it to pieces.

"If it's dangerous, why don't we just stop?" asked Felix.

"We can't just stop," I said. "Even if we lowered the sail, the tide would still carry us along. And we can't anchor in deep water. The anchor chain isn't long enough."

The sailor hauled in the weight and got ready to cast it again. He said, "As soon as we find the right depth of water, we'll drop anchor and wait for this blasted fog to clear. Keep your ears open, lads. Let me know if you hear the sound of waves breaking."

That made Felix keep quiet. We strained our ears for the sound that might mean land close by. I heard the creaks and groans of the ship, the slap of water against the hull, a seabird's mournful cry...

Oh, God, please guide us, I prayed. Bring us to a safe shore.

"There," whispered Felix, pointing into the mist. "Can't you hear it?"

At almost the same moment, the sailor shouted, "I've found bottom, Captain!"

"Drop anchor," the captain ordered. "Lower the sail. Jump to it!"

With a rattle of chains, the anchor dropped into the sea. The ship came to rest, rocking at the end of its anchor chain. Clearly through the fog came the sound of waves breaking on an invisible shore.

"Where are we?" Costicos asked again.

The captain gave him a cold stare. "We are somewhere off the southern coast of Britain. You should thank the gods that we've found a safe anchorage."

"How do you know it's safe?" Costicos demanded. "What if the wind changes? It's almost night. Don't you have the slightest idea where we are?"

"If you're asking me to make a guess, I'd say we're south of the island of Vectis. In that case the nearest decent harbour is Portus Ardaoni, on the mainland to the north. But I've no intention of wrecking my ship trying to find it. We'll stay here until the fog clears."

We ate supper without talking much. It was getting dark. The fog made everything feel cold and clammy. I began to shiver. This wasn't how I'd imagined my return to Britain.

The captain ordered one man to stay on deck, keeping watch. "Wake me at once if the wind rises," he said.

Everyone else went down below deck. The crew had their sleeping place in the stern, but there wasn't room there for passengers. We had to pick our way through the tightly packed hold to a small, empty space in the bow. The air was thick with the smells of wine, fish sauce and olive oil. Wrapping ourselves in our cloaks, we lay down and tried to get some sleep.

I don't know what it was that woke me in the depths of the night. A sound? The sudden jerk as something struck our hull? I sat up, wondering if the worst had happened and we'd hit a rock.

Then I heard a cry, quickly cut off, and the sound of running feet on the deck above.

"What's going on?" said Tiro, instantly awake.

The hold was very dark. I could hear confused movements at the far end, as the crew woke up. Suddenly, the main hatch was thrown open by someone up on deck. Candlelight flickered on fierce, bearded faces staring down into the hold.

"Pirates," Tiro whispered in my ear. "Don't move."

III

Night Attack

He didn't need to warn me. I was frozen with terror.

"How many?" asked one of the strangers.

"No more than half a dozen."

"Let's have them out, then." They were speaking my own language, with an accent I'd never heard before.

Their attention was on the crew. They didn't seem to notice us, crammed into our small, dark space behind the crates of cargo.

"Hey, you there!" one of them called to the sailors. "Come up on deck, one at a time. No weapons. There's far more of us than there are of you, so don't try anything."

The sailors, looking terrified, climbed the ladder one by one. The sound of footsteps told us they were being herded towards the stern of the ship. For the moment there was no one looking down on us.

"What's happening?" Costicos said, sleepily.

"Quiet!" I hissed.

"We think there are pirates on board," Tiro whispered. "But they don't know we're here. Keep down."

Suddenly, from up on deck, I heard a scream of pain. A moment later there came a splash as something hit the water. It sounded as if the pirates had knifed someone and thrown him in the sea.

My heart was pounding. I wanted to run, but where could we run to? If we climbed up on deck, the pirates would seize us instantly.

Oh, God... help us...

Another cry from above. Costicos let out a whimper of fear.

Crouching in the darkness, we had to listen helplessly to more screams. We soon realised that the entire crew was being butchered. But what could we do? We had no weapons, and there were only four of us against an unknown number of enemies. Soon it would be our turn. Soon they would find us.

I heard the tramp of feet returning towards the hatch. Again the light shone in. We pressed ourselves to the floor.

But it was the cargo that interested the raiders. One of them said, "Those look like wine jars."

"Our luck's in! Hoist one out and we'll see if you're right," said someone else.

We heard feet coming down the ladder. I tried to make myself small, silent and invisible under my cloak.

"It's wine all right," a voice shouted, and there was a roar of triumph. They heaved a large wine jar up onto the deck. Then they began to celebrate their victory, singing and drinking wine. The singing grew wilder as time went on. I couldn't make out all the words of the songs, or the things people said. Their accent was strange, and the more they drank, the more slurred their voices sounded.

"Isn't there any food on this leaking excuse for a ship?" someone demanded.

"Yes! Food! We're hungry!"

"Send the boy down to look for some."

"Where's the royal princeling? Where's the lord of the Brigantes? Send him to sniff out some food."

"Look at him - he's asleep. Wake up, kid!" There was a yelp of protest, as if an animal had been kicked in the belly.

A moment later, we heard cautious feet coming down the ladder. It sounded like just one person. He was holding a candle; shadows leaped and danced on the underside of the deck.

If he came this way, holding a light, he would certainly see us.

There was the sound of someone rummaging around near the stern, searching through the things the sailors had left behind. I didn't think he would find much food. After all, we hadn't been planning a long voyage.

Now the searcher was working his way forward, through the cluttered hold. I felt my hands tremble.

Oh, God, help us... hide us from the eyes of our enemies...

Closer and closer came the footsteps. I shut my eyes. Any moment now, there would be a shout of discovery. We would be dragged out and killed just like the others.

Then I heard, not a shout, but a small gasp of surprise. I looked up. Above the candle flame I saw the face of a young boy. He put his finger to his lips.

"Don't move," he mouthed. "Keep quiet."

I sat up, staring at him. I guessed his age was about 11 or 12. He had long, matted hair and his clothes were ragged. He looked as wild as the rest of the gang. But for some reason, he wasn't about to tell them we were here. Why not?

"Food. I need to give them some food," he whispered. "Or else they'll be down here looking for it."

Silently, I handed him the bag that held the remains of our food supply - some cheese and dried meat. We were all staring at him by now. I still couldn't believe that he might be on our side against the pirates.

"Stay still," he muttered. "I'll come back when they're all asleep."

He went back towards the ladder and began to climb it.

"What did he say?" whispered Tiro, for the boy had been speaking in the Celtic language, not Latin.

"He said to keep still until they're all asleep. He said he'd come back."

The boy was up on deck by now. I waited, tense, not knowing what to expect. But I need not have feared. He didn't give us away. I heard the pirates arguing over the food he had brought them.

"Well, that's all there is," said the boy. "Take a look yourself if you don't believe me."

"More wine, then!" came the cry. "Are we to die of thirst as well as starvation?"

More drinking, more singing... But gradually the noise grew less. I guessed that some of the pirates had fallen asleep.

Then, for what seemed ages, there were just two voices to be heard. They were talking about where they would take the wine to sell it. (Costicos cursed them under his breath.)

One of them said, "I can't believe our luck. We're not even looking for action. We're just trying to find a safe anchorage. And what happens? We run smack into a ship full of wine!"

"Didn't I tell you this would be a fortunate voyage?" said the other. "I tossed a coin into the sea as we set sail. That always brings luck."

"No, it's having the kid on board – that's what does it. And it's all thanks to me. I was the one who said we shouldn't kill him. The gods have smiled on us ever since."

At last their voices died down into silence. Had they fallen asleep? We had no way of knowing. It would mean death to venture up on deck if any of them were still awake.

Felix whispered, "Are we going to sit here all night? We've got to try and get out of here!"

"Wait a little longer," I said. "See if the boy comes back."

"He's probably fallen asleep like the rest of them," said Costicos. "Anyway, what makes you think we should trust him?"

"Shhh."

There was a creaking sound. Someone was climbing down the ladder. Then I heard a cautious whisper. It was the boy.

"If you want to get out of here, I can help you. But you must take me with you. I want to escape too."

Hurriedly, I translated this for Felix and Tiro.

"Tell him yes," said Tiro.

"Listen then," he said. "I'll go back on deck. You be ready at the foot of the ladder. If it's safe to come out, I'll tap twice on the deck, like this."

"Then what?" I asked him.

"Then we have to swim to shore. It's not far. The tide is almost at its lowest."

Costicos let out a despairing groan. I told Felix and Tiro what the boy had said.

"I'm not much of a swimmer," Felix muttered.

Neither was I. But what choice did we have? The sea might be more merciful than the pirates.

"Leave your cloaks behind," the boy whispered. "They'll only hinder you in the water. Are you ready, now?"

I swallowed hard. "We're ready."

IV

DEEP WATER

Balanced on a knife-edge of fear, I waited at the foot of the ladder. The sky above was dark – not a star to be seen. The fog must still be covering us like a damp, musty cloak. There was no sound except the wash of the waves.

Then we heard it – a quiet double tapping, like a rope knocking against the mast.

One by one, as silently as we could, we went up the ladder. A single, flickering candle showed the huddled shapes of men lying on the deck, and the black hull of the pirate ship anchored alongside. But I couldn't see the shore. Only the sound of the waves gave a clue to its direction.

What if those waves were breaking against a sheer cliff-face? What if I couldn't even get that far? An old fear gripped me – the fear of drowning. It had almost happened to me once. I could still remember my terrified struggles as the water overpowered me.

It wasn't the thought of death that scared me. Death, if you trust in God, is nothing to fear; it's the pathway to heaven. But I dreaded being swallowed up by water, with my breath giving out, my chest feeling as if it would burst...

No one seemed to want to be the first one making the jump. Then the young boy put us all to shame. He swung himself lightly over the side of the ship. For a moment I saw his two hands gripping the rail, and then they were gone. There was hardly a splash as he slid into the water.

Felix went next. Costicos hesitated until one of the pirates began to move restlessly and mutter in his sleep. That made up his mind for him.

Tiro took my arm, urging me on. I began to shake my head. I couldn't do it. I would stay here and take my chance with the pirates.

"Don't be afraid. I'll be right beside you," he said, so quietly I could hardly hear him.

"I can't. I just can't."

"Yes, you can."

Suddenly his strong arms scooped me off my feet and lifted me over the rail. Then he let me go, and I fell towards the sea.

Oh, the shock! The coldness of the water! I went under, then came up again. Somehow I managed not to cry out. Almost before I had time to panic, I felt a hand grab me. I couldn't see him in the dark, but yes, Tiro was there.

"Swim," he gasped. "Come on."

I hadn't swum in years. But my arms and legs remembered the movements learnt long ago, in the river near my village. I was afloat, my head was above water. The smooth waves lifted me like gentle hands. I almost laughed. Why had I been so frightened?

"This way," Tiro urged me, still close by my side.

As we swam closer to the sound of breaking waves, I began to feel scared again. There might be rough water ahead. And where were the others?

Then I saw a dark shape just in front of me. It was Felix, standing up in the water. I realised that we didn't have to swim any further. We were on a shelving beach; I could feel sand underfoot. The breakers, which had sounded so loud, were no more than waist deep.

At last we staggered to the shore. I was soaked and shivering. All my belongings were still on the ship, and I'd lost my sandals in the sea. But at least I was alive! I wanted to shout with relief.

"Is everyone safe?" asked Tiro. "Oh, thank God!"

All of us had made it to the shore. Costicos had collapsed in a heap on the sand. The boy stood beside him, looking impatient.

"Get up," he said. "We must be well away from here before daylight."

"Where are we to go?" I asked.

"Anywhere the pirates can't find me. I know they'll come looking for me."

Felix said, "Ask the boy if he knows where we are."

I asked him, and translated his answer.

"We're on an island. The pirates call it the Isle of White Cliffs. The mainland of Britain is to the north. But come on, we're wasting time! We have to get out of here!"

The boy was younger than all of us, and yet we found ourselves following his lead. On the far side of the beach, the ground sloped upwards into the darkness. All of us were shivering in our wet clothes. But there was no way of getting warm except to keep walking.

"Who are you?" I asked the boy. "Why were you with the pirates?"

"They captured me last year. They killed everyone else on board the ship, but they let me live. They think I bring them good luck on their voyages," he said, bitterly. "If they only knew the kind of luck I'd like to bring them!"

"Where do you come from?"

He didn't answer. He quickened his pace, as if he wanted to avoid my questions.

After a time, the darkness slowly changed to a misty, silver-grey light. We had climbed a hill and were coming down on the far side. The fog was starting to lift as the sun came up; we could see a little further ahead with each passing moment.

Then we heard dogs barking, and a cock's crow. That sounded to me as if we might be near a village. Soon, buildings came looming out of the fog: round, thatched huts like the homes of my own people.

What tribe would these people belong to? Would they speak my language? I had no idea. I just hoped they would be friendly to strangers.

***

Once they'd got over the shock of our arrival out of the mist, the villagers were quite kind to us. They led us into one of the huts, and made us sit close to the fire at its centre. A woman brought us some hot porridge. The children of the house stared at us, half-frightened, half-curious. It was Tiro who held their attention; I guessed they'd never seen a black man before.

Slowly, my cold bones began to thaw out. I closed my eyes, and could almost imagine I was back in my childhood home. This place was full of familiar smells – wood smoke, straw bedding, animals and food. It felt comforting and safe.

Felix was looking around him with interest. "So this is how the barbarians live," he whispered to me.

"This is how *I* used to live," I reminded him.

"A bit primitive, isn't it? And so dark and smoky. Don't your people like windows?"

"Shhh."

Costicos was talking to the men of the village, telling them our story. He was trying to persuade them to attack the pirates and rescue his cargo. But he wasn't having much success.

"There aren't enough of us," said one of the men. "And we don't have the weapons. The Romans don't allow us to have swords these days."

"Anyway, we don't want to make enemies of the pirates," said an old man. "They don't do us any harm at the moment. We leave them alone, they leave us alone."

Costicos didn't give up easily. "They've done *us* harm, though. Besides killing our captain and crew, they've stolen 100 amphorae of the best Falernian wine, and I want to get it back. If you help me, I'll give you ten amphorae. Do you know how much that's worth?"

I thought it was strange. A few hours ago he'd been afraid for his life. Now, instead of feeling glad that he'd survived, he was worrying about his possessions.

"The best thing you can do," said the old man, "is get yourself over to the mainland and tell the Romans. They hate the pirates. They've got ships patrolling the coast, seeking them out."

"But how am I to get there? I don't have a boat."

"I could take you in my fishing boat," said one of the men. "But that would mean I lose a day's fishing."

"Oh, I'll make it worth your while," said Costicos eagerly, and they began to haggle over the cost of the trip.

I told Felix and Tiro what was happening. "Maybe we could go too. But we'll have to pay for it." A nasty thought struck me. "What happened to our money?"

Tiro checked the pouch that was tied to his belt. Yes, the money was still safe, thank God.

We all went outside to have a look at the fishing boats. It was broad daylight now, and the mist had cleared. To the north of the village was open water, with land on the horizon. Several round-bottomed boats lay on the beach. They looked small and frail compared with the ship we'd been travelling on. But I couldn't see any other way of getting to the mainland.

While the bargaining went on, I felt a hand on my arm. The boy from the pirate ship was standing beside me.

"I don't want to stay here," he said, and then hesitated.

I guessed what he was trying to say, if only his pride would let him. "But you haven't any money. Right?"

He nodded.

"That's all right. We'll be happy to pay for you," I said, feeling sure Tiro would agree. "After all, you helped save our lives. Where are you heading for?"

"Nowhere. Anywhere."

He stared out across the water. His eyes looked as bleak and empty as the sea.

V

REVENGE

Very soon – though not soon enough to please
Costicos – two of the boats were made ready. We
waded out to them through the shallow water. Felix,
Tiro and Costicos got into one boat, leaving me to
travel in the other, along with the boy. Maybe this
would give me a chance to find out more about him.

He interested me. Why was he so secretive? Where
had he come from? And why didn't he want to go back
there?

When he spoke, he didn't sound at all like the
pirates. His accent was more like the speech of my
own people, though not quite the same. I looked at his
clothes, hoping for clues (every tribe has its own
pattern of cloth-weaving), but he wore only a ragged
tunic of sheepskin. He was too young to have the tribal
tattoos which boys are given when they become men.

I struggled to remember what the pirates had said about the boy. I was fairly sure the name "Brigantes" had been mentioned. The Brigantes were a fierce, warlike tribe who lived in the north and west. Their queen was an ally of the Romans, so they hadn't taken part in our rebellion. If they had, it might have ended differently.

Hadn't the pirates said something about a prince? But that must have been some kind of joke. The boy didn't look as if he had a spot of royal blood in him. He was filthy and ragged. His reddish hair hung in a tangle to his shoulders. His grey-green eyes seemed to flinch away if you looked at him too closely.

The wind was getting up; the fishing boats went scudding across the water, and soon the village looked small in the distance. I gazed back at the island, trying to see the bay where our ship was. The boy guessed what I was doing.

"You won't see it from here," he said. "It's on the far side of that point. The pirates always keep to the south side of the island. They lie in wait there for ships coming out from the mainland."

"What do you think they're doing now?" I asked him.

"Wishing they hadn't drunk so much wine!" he said. A grin slid over his face.

"And wondering where you've got to," I said.

At once he stopped smiling.

"Don't worry," I said. "They'll never find you now."

We were drawing closer to the mainland. I asked the fisherman the name of the port we were heading for.

"Portus Ardaoni, the Romans call it," he said.

"What was it called before the Romans came?"

"It wasn't called anything. There was nothing there until they started building their fort. But now... Well, you'll see."

The boy frowned at me. Then he said, "Aren't you a Roman?"

"Of course not! I'm a Celt of the Iceni tribe. I've lived in Rome, and I can speak Latin, but I'm not Roman."

"Really? You don't look like a Celt," he said, doubtfully.

I decided that before I met my family, I must get some different clothes to replace my Roman ones. That would be easy enough, but there were other changes that might not be so simple to make. I couldn't just forget everything that had happened to me since leaving Britain. I could never turn myself back into the person I used to be.

"Why did you go to Rome?" the fisherman asked.

I told him how I'd been captured after the great battle. "And now I'm going home. But I don't know if my home is still there."

"I hope you find what you're looking for," said the fisherman.

"You know all about me now," I said to the boy, "but I don't know the first thing about you. What's your name?"

He seemed to decide there was no harm in telling me that. "Don," he said.

"I'm Bryn. Which tribe do you belong to?"

"Mind your own business." His mouth set in a stubborn line.

We sailed through a narrow channel into a broad, calm bay, with low-lying land on three sides of us. Up ahead, several ships were moored close to the walls of a square-built fort. There was a small town, with a mixture of Roman and British-style buildings, red-tiled roofs and brown thatch.

"There. Quite a place, isn't it?" said the fisherman, admiringly. "And look – that's a warship of the Roman fleet tied up at the quay."

I saw Costicos, in the other boat, sit up suddenly. He was staring at the warship. It was worth looking at, with long, sleek lines, and a high prow which curved down to a vicious-looking ram. Even lying quietly at the quayside, it was threatening.

It seemed the ship was preparing to set out. The long oars were being put out through the oar-holes.

"Quickly!" I heard Costicos say to his boatman. "We must speak to the captain before he leaves port. If he knows where to look for the pirates, he might catch them unawares."

I looked doubtfully at Don. "Surely they won't still be there?"

"They might be. It will take them a good while to move all that cargo onto their own ship." I could see an almost feverish hatred in his eyes. "Romans against pirates – that's a battle I would love to watch! Let them hack each other to pieces! Let the seagulls peck out their eyes!"

***

Hours later, we were having a meal at a quayside inn, waiting for the warship to return. If the pirates had been defeated, we might have our belongings returned to us. And Costicos might get his wine back.

We had paid a visit to the public baths, to wash the salt off our skins. In the market we'd bought new shoes to replace the ones lost in the sea. With a good meal inside me, I began to feel normal again. It was safe here in the shadow of the Roman fort. I could forget the terrors of the last few hours.

Don looked far from relaxed, though. He was pacing up and down the quayside, looking out to sea. Suddenly he cried, "The Roman ship – it's coming back!"

The warship approached at speed, powered by the two banks of oars moving in perfect time. As it came to its mooring, I saw half a dozen bodies lying on the deck. They were pirates – not dead, I realised, but bound hand and foot. It seemed the Romans had won the battle.

"How many pirates were there altogether?" I asked Don.

"About twenty. The rest must have got away, or been killed. What will happen to the ones they've captured?"

"They'll be executed," said Costicos. "And a good thing too. They deserve to be crucified as a warning to others."

Don smiled. The Roman captain came down the gangplank, and Costicos hurried to meet him. "What's happened to my wine?" he demanded.

At first I thought the captain was going to walk right past, ignoring him. Then he seemed to remember that it was Costicos who'd tipped him off about the pirates. He gave him a grim smile.

"The merchant ship will be returning soon. Some of my men are on board. As far as I could see, most of the cargo is intact. As for the pirate vessel, we sank it. That's one ship that won't be making any more raids along this coast."

I looked to see if Don had understood the Latin words. But all his attention was on the pirates, who were being herded ashore by Roman guards. They looked miserable and scared.

Don ran alongside the men. "Hey, Finn! Do you feel lucky now? Did I bring you good fortune?"

One of the pirates swore at him. Don laughed.

"You're going to die," he taunted the men. "You're going to be crucified. You deserve it for all those men you killed, and for Aeron. It's your turn now! I hope you take a long time dying. May your wives and children starve!"

He did a triumphant war dance, shaking an imaginary spear at his enemies. The guards shoved him out of the way, but he followed them as they marched the pirates towards the gates of the fort. He was laughing and shouting insults at the captives.

"What's he saying?" asked Felix.

I translated some of Don's words – the less horrible ones. "I'm afraid that's what my people are like. If someone hurts us, we like to see them get paid back for it."

"But you're not like that," Felix said.

"Not now, I hope. But I used to be, before I was a Christian."

The guards and their captives went into the fort, where Don couldn't follow them. He came slowly back towards us, a gloating smile on his face.

Suddenly he looked uneasy, as if he could sense a hidden danger close by. He came to a stop. I thought he might be trying to say something, but the words came out as a meaningless gabble. Then his legs seemed to give way beneath him. He fell down on the stones of the quayside.

His arms and legs twitched uncontrollably. His eyes didn't seem to be looking at anything. Foam dribbled out of the corner of his mouth.

"What happened?" Felix gasped. He looked as shocked as I felt. "What's the matter with him?"

VI

THE FALLING SICKNESS

"Don't touch him," said Costicos, with fear in his voice. "The spirits of the dead have taken hold of him."

I was frightened too. It had all happened so fast. One moment Don seemed quite healthy - the next, he was twisting about on the ground. I didn't want to go near him in case the same thing happened to me. But Tiro had more courage than I had. He knelt down beside Don's shaking body, put a hand on his forehead, and prayed for him.

Two sailors paused as they went by.

"That looks like the falling sickness," one of them said.

The other agreed. "A mate of mine had it, years ago. He fell from the mast - that's how it started. He used to have turns like this every few days. In between times, he'd be perfectly fine."

"Couldn't the doctors do anything for him?"

"No."

Losing interest, they went away. By now, Don was lying still, as if deeply asleep. Either Tiro's prayer had helped him, or the strange fit had passed off, leaving him exhausted.

Costicos shuddered. "I knew there was something odd about that boy. The spirits have claimed him for their own. They may have left him for now, but they'll come back. It would be better not to have anything to do with him."

"The pirates thought he brought them luck," I said.

"Yes," said Felix, "and look what happened to them."

Before Don was fully awake, the merchant ship came into view, sailing across the bay. I couldn't help thinking about the men who'd been in command of it only yesterday. Now they were dead.

And we might so easily have been murdered too. One cry from Don when he discovered us – that's all it would have taken. Instead he had decided to help us. However strange and secretive he might be, we owed him our lives.

His eyes were open now. He moaned, and tried to sit up; then he fell back again.

"Tell him to lie still," said Tiro. "He mustn't try to get up until his strength comes back."

In our own language, I told him what Tiro had said. "You had the falling sickness," I added. "But you'll be all right."

Don looked up at Tiro, and I thought he looked puzzled.

Then Tiro said to me, "I've seen this sickness before. And I have seen it cured before, when people prayed in the name of Jesus."

I still felt a bit nervous. I'd never even heard of the falling sickness until now. But I guessed it had happened to Don before, and I wondered how people usually reacted. With fear? With disgust?

"Tiro," Felix called, "the ship's docked."

I stayed with Don while Tiro and Felix asked for permission to fetch our luggage from the ship. The sailors allowed this, but when Costicos tried to claim the cargo of wine, they told him he'd have to apply to their captain. "And you'll need proof that it belongs to you," he was told, "and money to pay the import taxes."

"You're worse than the pirates," Costicos complained.

A long argument began. We left them to it, for we had our own plans to discuss. Should we set out straight away to look for my home village? It would be a long journey. The Roman roads were good, but on foot we couldn't hope to travel far in a day. We didn't have money to spare for buying horses, and in any case, Felix had never learnt to ride.

We were talking in Latin, of course, but Don had been listening. I saw that he could understand some

Latin, even if he couldn't speak it. He asked me in our own language, "Did you say you're going to the land of the Iceni?"

"Yes."

"Which direction is that?"

"North-east, by way of Londinium. It's several days' journey." (I had found this out by asking questions in the market.)

"Can I go with you?" he asked.

"Of course, if you want to. But why? You're not from the Iceni tribe."

"No, but if your land is to the north, it must be on the way to... other places."

"To the land of the Brigantes?"

He gave me a startled glance. Then his face took on that closed, secretive look again.

I was getting tired of this. "Listen, Don, if you want to come with us, it's fine with me. But first I have to ask my friends what they think. We don't really know anything about you apart from your name. Can you tell me a bit more about yourself?"

He looked thoughtful. Then he seemed to decide he could trust me.

"All right," he said.

And so, sitting there at the quayside as the sun went down, he began to tell his story.

"You wouldn't guess it, looking at me now, but I was born into the royal family of the Brigantes. Queen Cartimandua had three sisters, and my mother was the youngest. My father, they say, was a great warrior, but

I don't remember him – he died in battle when I was very young.

"My mother told me that I took a long time being born, and they thought I might not live, but I survived. Then, when I was a few months old, I started having the... what you called the falling sickness. My own people had other names for it, and some of them thought I should have been left to die.

"The queen said, 'The gods have cursed him. He'll never be any use for anything. What good is a warrior who falls down before the first arrow is fired?'

"But my mother said, 'He's only a child. Maybe he'll grow out of this as he gets older.'

"When I was still young – six or seven, maybe – my mother found a new husband. She had another baby, but this time the child was born dead, and by nightfall my mother was dead too. I was taken into the care of her sister, the queen.

"I hated living in the royal household. The queen despised me. Other people laughed and called me names, but they were afraid when the spirits... I mean, when the sickness came upon me. My only friends were my cousins, Aeron and Merdyn. Aeron was a year older than me. He taught me to fight for myself and be brave, like a true son of the Brigantes.

"Our people have never been conquered by the Romans, because the queen made an alliance with them many years ago. She promised that if they left us alone, we wouldn't attack them. But the Romans didn't leave us alone. They built forts which threatened our borders. Worst of all, they gained power over our queen so that she was afraid to disobey them.

"In our tribe, the royal line runs through the women. When a queen marries, her husband becomes king. Anyway, Queen Cartimandua quarrelled with her husband and divorced him, but he raised an army to fight her for the throne. She called on the Romans for help – which is like inviting wolves in, to keep the fox away.

"The Romans defeated the king's army, but he escaped alive. He's still powerful in the northern lands of my tribe. The queen is afraid he'll attack again one day. She needs the help of the Romans to keep power, and she has to do whatever they ask her.

"Last year, the Roman governor sent a message to the queen. It was an invitation – an order, more like – to send three young princes to the court of the emperor. They would learn the language and ways of the Romans, and grow up to be friends of Rome.

"The queen didn't dare to disobey. She chose Aeron, Merdyn and me. I was chosen because she didn't care what happened to me. I don't know why she picked the other two. Perhaps it was because she had fallen out with their mother.

"None of us wanted to go. But we had no choice in the matter.

"Four Roman soldiers guarded us on our journey. They treated us like honoured guests. But really we were their prisoners. We travelled through the lands of different tribes, all under the rule of Rome... and we saw what that rule had done to them. They were like those fishermen today: no longer warriors. Their weapons had been taken from them. They relied on the Romans to protect them. And for this they paid taxes to the emperor. They had become his slaves!

"'That must never happen to the Brigantes,' Aeron said.

"At last we came to the sea. It was late in the year for sailing, but the Romans found a ship to take us across to Gaul. When we were halfway over, a sudden storm came up. The ship was blown westwards for a day and a night, unable to find harbour. As the sea grew calmer, we were beginning to thank the gods... But then the pirates attacked us.

"They outnumbered us completely, and they fought like wild beasts. Our four guards were no match for them. The pirates killed them, along with all the crew. After that it was our turn.

"At sword-point, we were stripped of our fine clothes and our gold. Their leader said it would be a shame to spill blood on such finery. Then Aeron and Merdyn were put to the sword. Both of them met death bravely, like warriors. The pirates would have killed me too – but the sickness took hold of me again.

"Maybe I should feel grateful to the spirits. They saved my life, for the pirates were frightened to kill me. But at the time, and for a long time after, I wished I had died with my friends."

VII

ON THE ROAD

Don couldn't go on with his story. Turning his face away, he got up and walked towards the end of the quay, where the warship was moored. Maybe he wanted to remind himself of what had happened to the pirates – they were all dead, or soon to die. There would be vengeance for the people they'd killed. But that wouldn't bring his friends back to life.

"What was he telling you?" Felix demanded.

I translated Don's story for Felix and Tiro, adding, "He asked if he could travel northwards with us. Is that all right? He hasn't got any money, though. We'd have to share our food with him."

Tiro nodded, but Felix looked doubtful.

"Do you actually believe his story?" he said. "All that about being a prince? He doesn't look much like one."

"A prince of the Brigantes isn't like the son of a Roman emperor," I reminded him. "And he's been with the pirates for months."

"So why didn't he try to escape from them?"

"I don't know. I'll ask him when he comes back."

"I don't trust him one little bit," Felix muttered. "He's probably after our money. We'll wake up one morning to find Tiro stabbed to death and all our money gone."

"Well, I *do* trust him," I said. "I don't think he could have made up a story like that."

Felix snorted. "He's a prince all right. A prince among storytellers."

But it was two against one. Tiro and I both thought we should let Don travel with us. Felix had to agree in the end.

Costicos, by now, had come to an agreement with the warship's captain. He was planning to hire ox carts and drivers to transport his cargo inland. People would pay better prices away from the seaport, he told us.

We said goodbye to him, wondering if our paths would ever cross again. Next morning, soon after sunrise, we set out on our journey.

***

The paved Roman roads made walking easy. They'd been built to allow soldiers to move quickly from one part of the country to another. Even in wet weather, they didn't turn into mud. But there was something wearying about the hard, straight line of the road. The trees had been cut back on either side, giving a long view into the distance. After seeing a town or a hilltop ahead, we seemed to take hours to reach it.

We passed the time by talking. Don was curious to know where Tiro had come from, and why his skin was so black. I told him how Tiro had been born in a distant land, away beyond the southern fringes of the Roman Empire. He'd been captured after a battle, taken to Rome by slave traders, and then given his freedom, years later.

"So Tiro isn't any more Roman than you are," said Don, sounding pleased. He pointed towards Felix. "What about *him*?"

"Felix is Roman, yes. But the emperor hates him – hates all of us, in fact."

"Why?"

"Because we are Christians. We believe there's only one God, and we don't worship the emperor. We almost got killed in Rome, on the emperor's orders."

I told him the story, hoping it would make him feel less hostile towards Felix. I could see the two of them didn't like each other much. Felix tried to be friendly; he knew that Christians aren't supposed to have enemies. But Don didn't bother to hide his dislike.

When I asked him, Don told me about his time with the pirates. They came from Hibernia, an island far to the west. When the autumn gales began, they went back there to spend the winter.

"How did they treat you?" I asked Don.

"Like a slave, most of the time. They were proud that a British prince was their servant. But then, when the sickness came on me, they'd feel wary of me again. I wished I could bring it on whenever I wanted!"

"Do you know when it's going to happen?" I asked him.

"Sometimes I feel strange, and I know I should lie down before I fall. Other times, it just happens with no warning at all."

Felix said, "Ask him why he never tried to escape from the pirates."

So I did.

"Of course I tried," said Don. "Not from Hibernia, because it was an island. How would I ever get back here? But when the pirates set sail again in the spring, they took me with them for good luck. One night when we were moored in a bay, I swam ashore. But Finn noticed I'd gone, curse him! They came after me and found me, because the sickness came on me again. Finn said it was a sign from the gods that I was meant to stay with them forever." He shivered.

I translated what Don had said.

Then Tiro asked, "What will he do now? Go back to his own people?"

But Don didn't seem to know the answer to that question. Suddenly, he looked small and helpless. "I don't know. If I do, the queen will send me to Rome. If I don't, where can I go? Strangers always fear me when they find out about my... my sickness... But *he* didn't," he said, looking at Tiro. "Ask him why he wasn't afraid."

"I'm not afraid of sickness, or the spirits of the dead, because I serve Jesus Christ, the Son of God," said Tiro. He began to tell Don the story of Jesus, stopping frequently so that I could translate what he said. It was a bit awkward, but Don kept listening, especially when we talked about Jesus making sick people well.

"I wish I could meet this Jesus," he said. "I would ask him to cure the falling sickness."

We told him how Jesus was crucified by the Romans, and how God raised him to life again. "He's in heaven now, but we can still pray in his name. Would you like us to pray for you?" I said.

"Yes," he said, eagerly.

So that night, when we stopped at an inn, Tiro asked for some oil. He spread it on Don's forehead, and we all prayed for him.

Felix said, "What if it's not a sickness? What if it really is an evil spirit inside him?"

"Lord, you know everything," Tiro prayed. "You know what is causing this. If it's a sickness, we ask you to heal it. If it's an evil spirit, then we cast it out in the name of Jesus!"

Don sat quite still, looking rather nervous. When we'd finished praying, he said, "I don't feel any different from before. How will I know if your God heard you?"

"You'll just have to wait and see," I said.

Should I warn him that not all prayers for healing were answered? I'd seen many people healed by God. I had also seen people who had prayed for a long time, but were not cured. It was hard to understand why.

"If a month goes by without the sickness coming on me, then I'll know I'm better," said Don, and suddenly he looked hopeful.

***

On the third day of our journey, we awoke to the sound of pouring rain. We decided not to set out unless the weather cleared up.

All day it rained. We sat in the inn, a dreary place with a leaking roof. Its owner was a grumpy man who seemed to hate his customers. The food we ordered, which took ages to arrive, was a greasy stew with lumps of gristle in it.

Felix groaned. "Why were you so keen to come back here?" he asked me. "The food is terrible, and so is the weather. And the natives aren't exactly friendly!" Don must have understood that bit – he gave Felix a hostile look.

"Rome isn't perfect either, you know," I said, and I pointed out a few things that were wrong with Felix's birthplace, from the emperor downwards.

We might have started quarrelling out of sheer boredom, but then Tiro suddenly said, "Bryn, I want to learn how to speak your language. Can you teach me?"

I stared at him. "Yes, I suppose so. Why do you want to learn?"

"Because ever since we arrived in Britain, I've had a feeling that this is where God wants me to be. Has anyone here even heard the name of Jesus? I would love to tell people about him. But it's very difficult if I don't know their language."

Felix looked horrified. "You can't mean it, Tiro! You really think God is calling you to this... this horrible, damp, half-civilised mud-hole? We're on the very edge of the empire here. We've already seen how dangerous it can be."

"No more dangerous for us than Rome under the rule of Nero," I reminded him.

"Wherever we go, we're in God's hands," said Tiro. "So teach me some of your language, Bryn. How do you say 'Greetings'?"

VIII

PAX ROMANA

Tiro was serious about learning the Celtic language. As we walked along the road, he kept asking me how to say things, and repeating them carefully. Don listened with interest. Sometimes he tried to correct Tiro's accent, which only confused him.

"Make your mind up. Do you want speak like the Iceni or the Brigantes?" I asked Tiro.

"I don't mind, as long as people can understand what I say."

Felix kept aloof from all this. He said he didn't want to learn a barbarian language; plain Latin was good enough for him.

On the following day we reached Londinium. The last time I saw the place, it was a blackened ruin, destroyed by the tribes who had rebelled against Rome. That was four years ago. Now I was amazed to see how the city had grown up again. Timber-framed warehouses lined the waterfront, where many ships were moored. Wooden shops and houses had been rebuilt after the fire. Everything looked new and rather rough at the edges; here and there, work was still going on. But Londinium was a city again, busy and prosperous.

We walked around, looking at the shops and market stalls. There were almost as many different things on sale as in the cities of Gaul. They came from every corner of the empire, and even beyond its borders... Greek vases, Samian bowls, Eastern spices, Iberian oil and Roman fish sauce... The list was endless.

"Not bad, this, for a half-civilised mud-hole on the edge of the empire," I said to Felix, and he grinned. He made me ask the prices of British goods, and noted them down for Septimus. Woollen cloth, leather, gold and silver, Celtic jewellery – all these were on sale, along with British slaves and even hunting dogs.

We didn't spend much money that day: there was no point in buying goods which we would have to transport with us. We bought Don some new clothes to replace his ragged tunic. And I couldn't resist buying a cloak and some breeches, woven in the pattern I remembered from my childhood. When I put them on, Don gave me an approving look. Felix frowned and said, "You're looking more and more like a barbarian."

"That's the whole idea. I don't want my family to look at me and see a Roman."

Of course, none of them might be alive to see me... I tried not to think about that.

***

We left Londinium the next day. At first, the land looked peaceful and prosperous. Around the villages, well-fed sheep and cattle were grazing. Good crops of corn had been planted.

"That's what happens when we civilise the barbarian tribes," said Felix. "We stop them fighting each other and killing each other off. We give them the peace of Rome. And they start to realise it's better to be farmers than warriors."

Don muttered something under his breath.

But as we travelled further north and east, things began to change. We had entered the land of the Trinovantes, who had taken part in the rebellion along with my own tribe. They had been punished for it. Four years later, the signs of that punishment could still be seen.

We passed the burnt-out remains of villages which had never been rebuilt. Perhaps there was no one to mend them because the people had been killed or enslaved. On land that had once been farmed, weeds were growing and wild deer were grazing.

There were other villages where life went on, except that there were hardly any men to be seen. Women and young children were doing the work of men. When we tried to buy food, there wasn't much to be had, and there were still months until harvest time.

I began to feel more and more afraid. What would I find in my own homeland?

One afternoon, a bad storm forced us to take shelter in a village. The people were wary of us at first.

But then a woman took pity on us and let us enter her hut.

"You belong to the Iceni?" she asked, looking at my cloak.

"Yes, but I haven't seen my homeland since the year of the great battle. I was captured and sold as a slave. Now I'm going home."

"Well, you'd better expect a few changes." She gave a harsh laugh. "From what I hear, the Iceni are even worse off than we are."

"You mean, because the Romans took revenge on them?"

She started to speak, then gave a frightened glance towards Felix.

"It's all right," I said. "He doesn't understand our language."

"The Romans are killing us," she said. "They killed our men in the great battle. Now they're killing the rest of us, making us pay taxes that we can't afford. You can see how little we have! Our children are hungry. But before we put food in their stomachs, we have to pay the fat-bellied tax collectors! And if we can't pay, our sons are taken away and sold."

I began to feel angry. "Are the Romans still taking revenge for the rebellion? It was four years ago. Haven't they punished us enough?"

"People say the Romans will never forget what Queen Boudicca did to them."

I had heard what our men did when they conquered Roman-built cities. Queen Boudicca had been tortured by the Romans. So her army took revenge by torturing the Roman women, before killing everyone and burning the cities to the ground. Now the Romans, in turn, were getting *their* revenge. When would it ever end?

Don had been listening. He looked furious.

"We should rise up against them!" he said. "We should all unite – all the tribes of Britain. Together, we can drive the Romans into the sea!"

"It's too late for that," the woman said, bitterly. "We have no warriors left here, only boys and old men. And no weapons, either. We are finished."

I felt relieved when the rain stopped and we could continue our journey. I didn't want to spend the night in that place of despair.

Before we set out, I told Felix and Tiro what the woman had said. "Can't we give her some money, Tiro? Enough to pay the tax collector next time?"

Tiro handed me a couple of silver coins. I ran back and gave them to the woman. She looked pleased for a moment, then embarrassed. "I have nothing to give you in return," she said.

Stupid of me – I'd forgotten one of the most basic customs of the Celts. I knew she would feel ashamed if she couldn't match my gift.

"No, no," I said. "You gave us shelter when we needed it. This is in return for your kindness."

The woman was looking around the hut. Then she went to her loom and picked up a piece of new-woven cloth. It would have taken her weeks to make – spinning the wool, dyeing it different colours, then weaving it into intricate patterns.

"I'm sorry this is worth so little," she said. "But I have nothing else I can give you."

"Worth so little! This is worth far more than what I gave you. In Londinium, I paid ten denarii for the cloak I'm wearing, and it's not as fine as this."

She stared at me. "The merchant who buys cloth from us never pays more than three denarii for a cloak. He says he can't pay more or he will lose money."

"He's lying, then," I said. "If he sells your cloth in the city, he'll make a fat profit. You should take it to Londinium and sell it yourself."

"How can I do that? Londinium is two days' journey away. I can't travel there and back just to sell a piece of cloth!"

"Then at least let me give you what this is really worth." I ran back to Tiro for some more money. At first I didn't think the woman would accept it, but she did. She was smiling as I said goodbye.

Felix looked at the cloth with great interest. "This is good quality. We could pay these people twice what they're getting now, and still cover the cost of the trip."

"Yes, and if the tax collector knows they're getting more money, he'll make them pay more taxes," I said, angrily. "They can't win, can they?"

"All right, all right," said Felix. "There's no need to shout at me. It's not my fault."

He was right, of course. I couldn't blame him for the wrongs of every Roman ever born.

"I'm sorry," I said. "But you can understand why I feel angry. How would you feel if you saw Romans being unfairly treated by the Celts?"

Tiro looked troubled. "Whatever nation we were born into, we are brothers – all children of the one Father. That's more important than Celt or Roman. Isn't it?"

"Yes," I muttered.

"Then let's make peace with each other and go on. Soon it will be nightfall."

IX

HOMELAND

The following day, we reached the land of my people, the Iceni. The woman was right – the Roman revenge had been terrible here, too. There were fields where even weeds did not grow; the land looked poisoned, as if it had been sown with salt. Nothing would grow there for years.

The road brought us to a small town beside a Roman fort. It was at the join of two rivers. I'd never seen the town before, but something about the lie of the land looked familiar. I felt as if I had been here before, a long time ago.

I tried to picture what this valley had looked like before the Romans built their fort. Was there a village there, between the two rivers? Yes... it was a place famous for its horses. We came here a few times when I was a child, and once Father bought a grey colt.

"I think I know this place," I said, excitedly. "If I'm right, my home village is further up that river."

"Can we get there before dark?" asked Felix.

"No, it's still miles away."

I was trying to stay calm. Half of me was impatient to get home; the other half was afraid of what I might find.

We spent that night in the town. The people here looked better off than the villagers, because the Romans from the fort had money to spend. A group of soldiers came into the inn as we were eating our meal. They looked at us curiously. One of them asked Felix – the most Roman-looking of us – what our business was. Felix told them he was a trader.

"And your native friends?" the soldier said, staring at Don and me. "I suppose they're your interpreters? Well, a word of warning, son..." And he muttered something to Felix.

"Never trust the British," said one of the others. "You think you've got them under control, and then, as soon as you turn your back, they'll stick a knife in it."

"There's trouble brewing in the north at the moment, I hear," the first soldier said to Felix. "So don't go too far north in your travels. But you'll be safe enough hereabouts, among the Iceni. We've pacified them all right." And he laughed.

"Pacified them," said Felix. "Is that what you call it? Crushed them into the ground, it looks like."

"Well, we can't take any chances. They must never rebel again like they did four years ago."

"It doesn't look as if they have any warriors left to fight," said Felix. "I think we should treat them more gently now that they are defeated. Then, maybe, their children won't grow up to hate us."

"Listen to the young philosopher," the soldier said, mockingly. "You've never been in the army, son, or you wouldn't talk like that. A firm hand – that's what the British tribes understand best."

I couldn't stay silent any longer. "There's a difference between a firm hand and a rod across our backs. Why are you making our people pay such heavy taxes?"

"Oh, taxes – that's not up to us," said one of the men. "It's the procurator who decides all that."

I said, "Well, the procurator should know that by taxing people so cruelly, he'll stir up another rebellion. It would be better to treat our people with fairness."

"Oh, yes? And who's going to rebel – the women and old men?"

I wanted to say the boys who are growing up now, learning to hate all Romans! But Tiro had put his hand on my arm, silently telling me: calm down. Don't let them think you're a troublemaker.

Another soldier said, "They say a new procurator has been appointed, so you may be lucky, boy. He may be more lenient than the old one."

"Never mind him – it's a new governor that we need," said the first soldier. "One who'll take the northern tribes in hand. It's high time we taught the Brigantes a lesson."

The word "Brigantes" made Don look up. But nothing more was said on the subject. The conversation changed to the sort of things soldiers always talk about – women and food and lousy pay.

Next day, I was still feeling angry. The Romans were so arrogant! They thought the whole world was theirs to conquer and rule over. And anyone who got in their way was simply crushed, like a beetle under a cartwheel.

At least Felix wasn't like the rest of them. I was grateful to him for trying to speak up for the British. But it had been pointless; it wouldn't change anything.

By now we were heading westwards, up the valley of a slow-moving river. My village stood – or used to stand – on a low hill in a loop of the river. We should reach it by noon. I felt as if there was a tight knot in my stomach, growing tighter with every mile.

"What were the soldiers saying about my people?" Don asked me, so I told him the little I'd heard. Trouble brewing in the north; I wondered what that meant.

"Maybe King Venutius has grown powerful again," said Don. "He hates his ex-wife, Queen Cartimandua, but he hates the Romans even more. Do you know how far we are from the lands of the Brigantes?"

I shook my head. I had only the vaguest idea about the country beyond the boundaries of my own tribe. A tribe called the Corieltauvi lived to the north-west of us, and then, somewhere beyond them, the Brigantes. I guessed it would be several days' journey to their territory.

"What are you going to do? Return to your people?" I asked Don.

"Yes. If they are going to war with the Romans, then I want to be there!" he said fiercely.

"You'd make the journey on your own?" It was a stupid question, I realised as I said it. Don might be young, but he was tough. His weakness was the falling sickness which could attack him like a hidden enemy. But since we had prayed for him, he hadn't had another attack.

He gave me a thoughtful look. "You could come with me," he said. "If you don't find your family, I mean."

"No," I said. "If I don't find my family, I'll go back to Gaul with my friends."

"What, and become a tame Celt again – a slave of the Romans?" he said scornfully.

I didn't answer, for we had come to a place I knew. This ford across the river – I must have crossed it dozens of times. I had fished in the brown pool below. I'd helped my brother to herd sheep on that hillside. I was almost home.

Another bend of the river, and there was the village. It stood on its small hill, exactly as I remembered it: a cluster of round, thatched huts, each with a thin trail of smoke going up into the sky.

Many times over, I'd imagined this moment. I had often dreamed about it, only to wake up feeling lost and desolate. Now it was really happening. I was coming home at last.

But what if there was no one here that I knew? If none of my family had survived, this wouldn't be home. It would be just a village and a few old memories.

"Wait here by the river," I told the others. "I don't know who lives in the village now. They may not be friendly to strangers."

In my dreams, I always raced up the hill, faster than a running deer. Now that the moment had finally arrived, I walked up slowly, hardly daring to hope. I'd come so far... I'd waited so long...

At the door of my old home, I paused for a moment. Then I took a deep breath and went in.

In the dim, smoky light I saw a woman stirring a pot by the fire. She was thin and grey-haired. For an instant I thought she was my grandmother... but Grandmother had died years ago.

The woman looked up. "Is that you, Conan?" she asked.

Conan was my brother's name. Maybe I had grown up to look like him. "It's not Conan," I said. "It's Bryn."

She cried out as if someone had stabbed her. Then she ran to me, and looked up at me, and started laughing and weeping both at once. "Bryn! Oh, Bryn, is it really you? I never thought I'd see you again!"

She hugged me, and that was when I knew for certain – she was my mother.

All the longings of the last four years... all the sorrow and pain... all the lost memories welled up inside me, until I thought my heart would burst. I couldn't say a word.

Fortunately, Mother had words enough for both of us. "Are you all right? Here, sit down by the fire. How did you get here? However did you escape from Rome? You must be hungry – I'll get you some food."

Feeling dazed, I sat down. My home was just as I remembered it, except that it looked smaller somehow, because I had grown bigger.

I was home again. I couldn't quite believe it – home at last.

X

WELCOME

There was a movement in the doorway behind me. A girl came in, carrying a water jar. It took me a moment or two to be sure, for I hadn't seen my sister since she was 6. But I recognised her freckled face and red-gold hair.

"This must be Enid," I said.

"It's Bryn," Mother told her. "He's come back to us!"

Enid didn't run towards me as Mother had done. She put the water jar down carefully and looked me up and down. She said to Mother, "Are you sure it's really him?"

"Maybe I look different," I said. "So do you. But I remember you all right. Do you still have your tame blackbird? And the grey kitten that you found in the woods?"

"The blackbird died. And the kitten's grown up and had kittens of her own." She came closer, still watchful. Then suddenly she smiled. "It *is* you! Conan always said you'd find your way home."

"Conan! So he got back here all right! Where is he?" I demanded.

"He's gone off on one of his journeys," said Mother. "He can't seem to settle down. Two years and more he's been back, but he's still restless. He should find himself a wife, that's what I keep telling him."

"Where did he go?" I asked.

"I don't know. He set out westwards just before lambing time. He said he'd be back by Beltane, but he hasn't arrived."

Beltane was the spring festival. It must have been more than two months ago.

"Are you worried about him?" I asked Mother.

"It's no good worrying. And it's no good telling him we need him here. He never listens. When the restlessness takes hold of him, nothing will keep him in the village."

I thought I could understand how he felt. Four years ago, he'd been snatched away from his homeland. He had been sold as a slave in Rome. He'd trained as a gladiator and fought in the arena. Then, somehow, he'd found his way back here, halfway across the empire. How could he settle down to a peaceful life of farming, as if none of that had ever happened?

"He just doesn't think," said Enid, angrily. "He left us to take care of the lambing on our own, and the spring ploughing. Ploughing isn't women's work! We did what we could, but this year's harvest won't be anything like last year's."

"Aren't there any other men in the village to help?" I asked, already guessing the answer.

"Only old Evan and Lloyd," said Enid. "One's lame and the other's half-blind."

Mother said wearily, "Hardly any of the men came back after the great battle. Maybe some are still alive somewhere – taken away as slaves, like you and Conan. We don't know. We think most of them were killed by the Romans."

I could still picture that terrible battlefield, where dead men lay like stones on a beach, too many to count... Dead women and children too. But Mother had escaped with my two sisters before the final defeat.

"You were lucky to get away when you did," I said. "Hey, where's Bronwen?"

A shadow came over my mother's face. "She didn't live through that winter. That was a bad time. No harvest, hardly any food, and many people died... Oh, Bronwen, my little one! I wish you were here to see your brother come home!"

She was weeping. Although I could hardly remember my little sister's face, I wanted to weep too. I wanted to cry for all the lost lives and broken families, and the ruin caused by war. I'd been a fool to think I could come back and find that everything would be like it used to be. That life was gone for ever.

I put my arms around Mother. It felt strange that I was taller than her now; old enough to try and comfort her as she used to comfort me.

Enid said, "Who are those people down by the river? Do you know them, Bryn? There's one who looks like a Roman. And one is in Roman clothes, but his face is as black as moleskin."

Feeling guilty – I'd totally forgotten about my friends – I told Mother about them. "Felix *is* a Roman," I admitted, "but he helped to save my life once. Not all Romans are bad."

"Bring them in," Mother said. "If they are your friends, they're welcome here."

***

That night she cooked a special meal, and invited the whole village. It wasn't like the great feasts I remembered from my childhood, for food was much scarcer now. But she killed a sheep to roast over the fire, and there was enough meat for everyone. The village now held only about thirty people – less than half the size it used to be.

Feasts were always a time for storytelling in the glow of the firelight. That night, instead of the old legends about heroes and warriors, we told stories which were almost as amazing, but true. Don told of his time with the pirates. I talked about my life as a slave in Rome, and how Tiro had saved me by buying my freedom. How we had all been arrested by the emperor's men. How Felix had helped us to escape...

I wanted people to understand that Tiro and Felix, although not from our tribe, were as close to me as brothers. I knew that my people were suspicious of strangers, especially strangers in Roman clothes, who spoke Latin among themselves.

Tiro now understood a little of our language – enough to follow some of what I said.

"You haven't told them the most important thing," he said to me in Latin.

"What do you mean?"

"The reason we were arrested. Our faith in God."

"Well, no," I said awkwardly. "Not yet. I don't want them to think I've changed too much, turned into a foreigner."

"Will you let me tell them? They already know I'm a foreigner," he said, grinning. "You'll have to translate for me, though."

He told of growing up in a far southern land, under a burning hot sun. The people of his tribe were hunters and warriors. (Here he got up and danced as they used to dance, stamping his feet and pretending to shake a spear. It looked rather like the war dance of my own tribe.) After a battle between two tribes, he was captured and sold as a slave. He ended up in Rome, serving a cruel master.

"I hated him," he said. "I hated all the Romans. I tried to run away, but I was caught and punished. My hatred blazed inside me like a flame. I would have killed my master if I thought I could get away with it."

There were murmurs of sympathy as I translated this. Everyone, from the oldest to the youngest, was listening.

"One day my master bought a new slave. His name was Zedekiah. He came from a land in the east, and his religion was a very strange one, I thought. He believed there was only one God. And this God wanted people to love each other, not hate one another. So if someone hurt Zedekiah, he didn't try to get his own back. I had never met anyone like him.

"Another slave broke the master's favourite wine cup one day. He was afraid of being punished, so he told the master that Zedekiah had done it. Zedekiah said nothing. He got a terrible beating, even though he hadn't done anything.

"Afterwards, I told him he was crazy. But he said, 'I'm only following in the footsteps of Jesus, God's Son. He came to earth to show us how much God loves us. And he was killed, even though he didn't deserve it – he took our punishment, so that we could walk free.'"

Tiro went on to talk about how he came to believe in this loving God. He stopped hating his enemies and tried to love them instead. But as I translated his words, I could see puzzled looks amongst the audience. I knew it all seemed very strange to them. Hatred and revenge, they understood. Loving your enemies? That, to them, was pure madness.

When Tiro stopped talking, someone cried, "Let's have a song!" The evening became noisy again. I joined in the singing, when I could remember the words. The songs were all about battles and the brave deeds of heroes. There was one which had been my father's favourite. I couldn't bring myself to sing that one.

If only the Romans had never come to Britain! If only they had left us alone! Father would still be alive, along with Bronwen and all the others who had died so needlessly. Our family would still be together. This village would not be a half-empty shell. It was all the fault of the Romans, with their arrogance and greed.

Loving your enemies – Tiro had made it sound so easy. I thought it was the hardest thing on earth.

XI

HAYMAKING

"Now what?" said Felix, the next day.

"What do you mean?" I asked him.

"Well, you've found your old home. That's what you wanted to do. Are you going to settle down here for the rest of your life?"

He obviously didn't think it would be much of a life. Although he'd managed not to complain out loud, he wasn't impressed by my home – a one-roomed hut with straw for bedding. (He was still picking bits of straw out of his hair.)

He looked up at the roof. "By the way, what are those things sitting on the rafters up there? The household gods? They almost look like dried-up human heads."

I said, "That's exactly what they are – the heads of enemies killed in battle. But don't worry, Felix. You're our guest. Your head isn't going to end up there." He seemed to think I was joking.

I should have known Felix wouldn't like my home village. As well as no beds, it had no bath house, no running water, no Roman-style food... no civilisation, in fact. Of course, I didn't mind any of that. It was like returning to my childhood. But I wasn't sure I could live here forever, far away from my Christian friends. Life would be difficult if I had no one to pray and worship with.

Tiro said, "You must ask God what he wants you to do. Pray, and God will guide you."

I said, "I know I should stay here for the summer, at least. Mother and Enid need me. There's the haymaking and the corn harvest – they need extra hands to help with all that. If they don't get enough corn and hay, it will be a hard winter."

"What's hay?" asked Felix. You couldn't blame him for his ignorance – he had always lived in cities.

I said, "It's dried grass to feed the animals in wintertime. If we don't harvest enough of it, our sheep and cattle will starve. The hay's almost ready for cutting, if the weather stays dry."

Tiro said, "I can help, if you want."

Felix and Tiro decided they would both help. When the haymaking was over, they would start to travel around the villages, looking for woollen cloth to buy.

"We'll need some kind of transport," said Felix. "Oxen or packhorses."

"Packhorses," said Tiro at once. He'd spent years working with horses and knew their ways. "Buy them around here, then sell them before you set sail for Gaul, Felix."

"Won't you be coming back with me?" said Felix.

"I don't know yet. I must do the same as Bryn – pray for God's guidance."

As for Don, I half-expected him to set off north-westwards, looking for his own people. But something happened to stop him. The falling sickness struck him again.

It happened when we were down at the river, having a wash after a hot day in the fields. Our bathing place was a cool, rippling river pool – far better than a Roman bath house, I thought. Felix didn't agree.

"Ow! It's cold," he gasped. "Tell them to put more wood on the fire!"

"Romans are soft," Don jeered. He swam across to the other side, then turned to come back. That was when I noticed the strange, anxious look on his face. He stopped swimming, stood up... then collapsed into the water.

"Tiro! Help!" I cried.

We heaved Don out onto the riverbank. He'd only been under water for a few moments. It was just like before – his body was twitching violently, his mind had gone somewhere far away.

Tiro prayed for him again. After a time, the violent movements stopped, and Don seemed to go to sleep.

"I thought God had healed him," I said, disappointed. "But he's just as bad as before."

Felix said, "I really thought he might start to believe in God. Now he'll think we were talking nonsense. Why didn't God heal him properly?"

"I don't know," said Tiro, looking troubled. "God doesn't always give us everything we ask for. You know that."

Two boys from the village had seen what happened. I heard them mutter something about "evil spirits" as they ran off to spread the news. Oh, no - that was the last thing we needed. People were already suspicious of us for being too foreign, too Roman, too weird...

When Don woke up, he realised what had happened. But he didn't seem surprised.

"I thought it was too good to be true," he said. "The druids couldn't cure me, even with the sacrifice of a pure white bull. How could you make me better just by saying prayers? It's no use. I will always be like this."

***

As the days went on, and we worked hard at the haymaking, the villagers became more friendly. They liked Tiro's attempts to speak their language. It amazed them that Felix was prepared to work alongside them, even though he was Roman. (They hadn't met many Romans up to now - only soldiers and tax officials.)

All day, Felix, Tiro and I went back and forth across the hay fields, cutting the long grass with scythes. It was hard work; our hands got blistered at first, but after a few days they toughened up.

Behind us, Don and the other youngsters raked the grass into rows and left it to dry. Fortunately the weather stayed fair. After a few days, the hay was carted back to the village. Old Evan and Lloyd built it up into haystacks, with sloping, thatched tops almost like roofs, to keep the rain out.

"You'd better learn how to do this job," Evan said to me. "Who else will know about it when we're dead and gone?"

Part of me was pleased by this – Evan spoke as if I belonged here. But part of me felt unsure about the future. Did I really *want* to belong here, to live out my life and grow old in the village? The world was so much wider than this valley.

The fine weather lasted until all the hay was in. Then it broke, with thunderstorms and heavy rain. But it didn't matter. Eight good, big haystacks stood ready for the winter. Mother said it was the best haymaking since before the rebellion.

"And that's thanks to you and your friends," she told me. "Will they still be here for the corn harvest?"

"I don't know. What they really want to do is to trade, and so far we haven't bought a thing."

Next day, we went down river to the town, where we bought two packhorses. They were scruffy-looking animals, but Tiro said they seemed healthy enough. We also bought enough grain to feed the village until the corn was ripe. People couldn't live on hay, and the corn pits were almost empty.

In the quiet spell between haymaking and harvest time, we began trading. We travelled to the neighbouring villages, offering to buy spun wool and woollen cloth. We paid better prices than the merchants who had been round that way before, so people were happy to sell to us. My own village was our base; we brought all the goods back there.

Tiro was getting more confident in speaking our language. He could manage to bargain for things without much help from me. Also, when he got the chance, he would tell people about Jesus. And people listened, much to my surprise.

"They're hungry," said Tiro. "Their hearts are hungry for the good news."

"Be careful," I warned him. "The druids won't like it if they think you're leading people away from their gods."

"The druids are your people's priests, aren't they? Where are these druids?" asked Felix. "I've never seen one."

"Most of them have gone into hiding in the forests and marshes. The Romans want to drive them out. But they're still powerful, my mother says."

I had tried to talk to Mother and Enid about God. They looked at me doubtfully. They couldn't see why I had stopped believing in the gods of my people – Lugh, Camulos, Andraste, and all the rest.

"Now that you're back home, you should forget this foreign god of yours," Mother said. "Remember the gods we always worshipped. They're all around us, in the woods and the river and the stars and the sun. If we honour them, they'll protect us. But if we ignore them, we'll make them angry."

"Did those gods really help you when you prayed to them?" I asked. "Did they bring you food in the bad winter?"

"No," Mother admitted. "The druid said it was because we didn't make enough offerings."

I said, "My God doesn't demand offerings. I can pray to him anytime, wherever I am. He's greater than the woods and rivers and sun and stars – he created all of them."

Enid said, "If you ask him for something, will he do it?"

"Often he does. Not always," I said, thinking of Don. "Is there something you want me to pray for?"

"Pray that Conan comes back safe," she said. "But I don't believe it will happen. He's been gone for months now. Somehow I don't think he's ever coming back."

XII

WAR IN THE NORTH

It was while we were out on our travels that the tax collector came.

The first we knew of it was when we returned from a two-day trip towards the coast. It had been a successful journey; the packhorses were loaded with bundles of cloth. As we came in sight of the village, Enid came running to meet us.

"They took your things!" she gasped. "We couldn't stop them! We couldn't pay, so they took whatever they wanted. I want to kill them!" She was shaking with fury.

"Hold on a minute," I said. "Calm down. Before you start killing people, tell us what happened."

"It was the tax collector. He came early – usually he arrives after harvest time. He looks at how much grain we have in the storage pits, and he makes us pay tax on it. Last year he was angry because there wasn't very much, and he said we'd hidden our harvest to cheat the emperor. But why should we pay tax to the emperor? These are *our* fields. The corn is *ours*. If the emperor wants corn, let him plant it himself!"

"I suppose this tax man is a Roman," Don said, angrily.

"No, he's from our own tribe, but he has a troop of Roman soldiers to protect him. The coward! The traitor! May his own children spit on his grave!"

"Didn't you show him how little corn there is to harvest?" Tiro asked her.

"Yes – Evan showed him the fields, and said that we'll have barely enough corn to get us through the winter. The tax collector called us idle and lazy. He said if we couldn't pay, he would take some of us as slaves. Then the soldiers marched into the house as if they owned it, and they found your store of cloth, and took half of it. I'm sorry! We just couldn't stop them!"

I told Felix what had happened. He looked furious. "They've no right to do that," he said. "We must complain to the procurator! If only we'd been here when they arrived!"

I didn't think it would have made much difference whether we were there or not. What could we do against a troop of soldiers?

"They didn't take anyone captive, did they?" Tiro asked.

"No, they said the cloth would be enough payment. Until the next time, that is," Enid said bitterly. "Until they come back next year, wanting more. I hate them!"

I felt angry too. We'd bought that cloth with money which wasn't really ours – it had been lent to us by Septimus. Would we ever be able to repay him?

But when I saw how upset Mother was, I managed to stay calm. "It doesn't matter," I told her. "We can easily buy some more. Don't worry about it!"

***

Early in the morning, I was awakened by the growling of a dog. I got up cautiously. Was there someone outside?

The door opened quietly. The dog stopped growling and began to wag his tail. A tall man stood in the doorway, dark against the pale dawn light.

"Conan," I whispered.

He froze. "Who's there?"

"It's me. Bryn."

I heard him gasp in amazement; then he crossed the room in three strides.

"Bryn! Good to see you, brother." He gripped me by the shoulders. "You've grown tall since I saw you last."

Conan was four years older than I was. I had almost caught up to him in height, but he looked far tougher and stronger than me. He had grown into a man. I still felt like what I'd always been – his little brother.

"Are you all right?" he asked.

"I'm fine. Are *you* all right? Mother was worried about you. Where have you been?"

"Around and about," he said. "Is there any food in the house? I'm starving, and so are my men."

"What do you mean, your men?"

He didn't answer me. He went over to Mother's sleeping place and shook her awake. When she'd got over her joy at seeing him, he asked again for food.

"There's a pot of porridge that's been cooking overnight," she said.

"That won't be enough," said Conan. "There are 50 warriors hiding in the woods across the valley. I need all the food you've got. It's only for today, Mother – we'll be on our way again tonight."

"Conan, tell me what's going on," said Mother.

By now, the others were waking up. Conan looked startled to find strangers in his house.

"Who's this? Your brother?" Felix asked me, speaking Latin, of course.

"What are those Romans doing here?" Conan hissed.

"These are my friends," I said. "Remember Tiro? You met him in Rome, years ago. And this is Felix, and Don. Meet my brother, Conan."

Conan greeted them politely enough in our own tongue, but I could tell he was angry. Just a few words of Latin were enough to set his teeth on edge. He'd always hated Rome and everything Roman.

"Tiro comes from Africa," I reminded him. "And Don belongs to the Brigantes. As for Felix, he may be

Roman, but you can trust him all right. He's a good friend."

Conan gave me a disbelieving look. "Come outside, Mother, there's something I have to tell you," he said.

When Mother came back, she was alone. She told Enid to fetch some water. Then she started preparing to make bread – an enormous batch of bread.

"What's going on?" I asked her.

"I'm not supposed to say." Her face was troubled.

"I heard something about 50 warriors hiding in the woods. Is it true?"

She nodded. "How am I to feed them all, without any warning? First the tax collector, now Conan and his men. I'm like grain being crushed between two millstones."

Enid brought the water jar. "Has Conan come home, then?" she asked.

"He's come back, but only to get food," Mother said, angrily. "He won't stay to help us with the harvest. He says there are more important things to deal with. What's more important than helping us live through the winter?"

"I can guess," I said. "He wants to fight the Romans." I saw by Mother's face that my guess was correct.

"With 50 men?" said Don. "He must be a fool."

Mother sighed. "He says there's an army gathering in the north-west. He's been trying to persuade our people to join it. He'll want you to go too, Bryn. Don't listen to him! He'll get himself killed, just like your father did."

Don's face was alight with interest. "An army in the north-west... Would that be among my people, the Brigantes?"

But Mother didn't know. "Ask him, when he comes back," she said. "He's going around the village trying to get more food for his men."

While we were eating breakfast, Conan returned. He ate hungrily, as if he hadn't had a good meal for days.

"Tell me about this gathering in the north," said Don. "Are my people going to rise up and fight?"

Conan shot Mother an angry look. "I told you not to say anything in front of the Roman!"

"Don't worry," I said. "Felix doesn't know our language."

"Never trust a Roman," Conan muttered.

Don said, "I bet it's King Venutius who's raising the army. He hates the Romans because they helped Queen Cartimandua to stay in power. Am I right?"

Conan stared at him. "How do you know so much about it?"

"My mother was the sister of Queen Cartimandua," Don said, calmly. "But don't worry – I'm not on the queen's side. I hate her! I'd fight for Venutius any day."

"Let me get this right," I said. "One half of the Brigantes are preparing to fight the other half, and the Roman army. I'd say the rebels haven't got a chance."

"That's why we're trying to rouse the other British tribes to join the war," said Conan. "This is our chance to get rid of the Romans. We'll drive them out for ever! We'll have our revenge for what they've done to us, and the land will be ours again. Bryn, are you with us? We need you. We need everyone who can hold a spear."

XIII

TIME TO GO

I didn't know what to say. My thoughts were all mixed up, like a river after cows have been trampling in it, stirring up clouds of mud.

Part of me wanted to shout, "Yes! Of course I'll join you. Death to all Romans! They deserve it for what they've done to us!"

Another part of me was more cautious. I felt pleased that Conan wanted my help – but what could I do? I wasn't a fighter like he was. At the time when he was being trained as a gladiator, I worked in a Roman kitchen. In my childhood I'd started learning how to use a sword and spear, but that was long ago.

And another voice spoke to me quietly: Wait a moment. Think about this. What would God want you to do?

"Well?" said Conan, impatiently. "Are you with us, or not?"

Enid's eyes were shining. She said, "I'd go! If I was old enough, I'd go and fight!" And I heard Mother moan with dismay.

"I don't know," I said. "Give me some time to think about it. When are you leaving?"

"After dark tonight. We don't want the Romans to see us on the move."

"They already know there's something going on," I said, and I told him what the soldiers had said about trouble brewing in the north.

"So they know. It doesn't matter," Conan said. "If we can gather all the tribes against them, we can easily defeat them. We'll have far more men than they have."

"That's what everyone said before the last great battle," I reminded him. "But the Romans still won."

He stared at me. "I'm starting to wonder whose side you're on. What are you – a Celt or a Roman?"

I didn't have to answer that, because Don interrupted. "Take me with you," he begged Conan. "I can fight if you give me a sword. And I know the ways of my own tribe. I can help you on your journey."

"How old are you?" Conan asked him.

"Nearly 13."

Conan looked him over, then nodded. "You can come. Aren't you ashamed, Bryn? This kid has more courage than you have."

"It's not that I'm scared," I said. (Not quite truthfully. I couldn't forget that battle, when the Roman legion carved through our warriors like a knife slitting a fish.) "But what will happen to the harvest if we go off to war?"

"We'll get a much better harvest than this!" said Conan. "We'll harvest the Roman grain stores and take back everything they've stolen from us!"

Mother said bitterly, "That's what the men said in the year of the rebellion. That's why people starved the following winter. Don't go, Bryn! We need you here!"

Unsure of what to do, I glanced from Mother to Conan. There was no way of pleasing them both. I looked to Tiro for help.

"Did you understand what Conan said?" I asked him.

"Most of it. And I understand your longing to fight for your people. But Bryn... think what Jesus would do."

Conan didn't like the fact that we were speaking in Latin. "You *are* a Roman," he said to me, scornfully. "You're a traitor to your own people – either that or a coward. Stay at home, then, and spin wool with the women. We don't need people like you."

"No!" I cried, suddenly making my mind up. "I'll go with you. What do I need to bring?"

"Whatever weapons we've got. There's a dagger and a couple of hunting spears hidden in the roof thatch. And whose are those packhorses I saw in the meadow? They could be useful."

"They don't belong to me," I said. "Felix needs them."

Poor Felix was looking bewildered. He still didn't know what was going on. Tiro would have to explain it to him.

"But first of all, the food," Conan said. "You can help me carry it to our camp. Is the bread ready yet, Mother?"

Mother nodded silently. Her face was like stone.

***

What Conan had called a camp was just a huddle of rough shelters in the woods. Most of his people were asleep; they had been travelling all night. But they soon awoke when Conan called, "Food!"

They were all ravenous. The food from the village quickly disappeared, and people looked hungrily through the trees to the pasture where sheep were grazing.

"The village should give us a sheep for an offering to Camulos," said one of the men. He had a long beard, like a druid. Maybe he was a druid, although he wore ordinary, rather ragged clothes.

"If they won't give us one, we'll take it!" cried a young man, and others agreed with him.

"No," said Conan. "These are my people. We don't steal from them – understood?"

There was some muttering, but no one argued with him. He was the leader. I saw that his "warriors" were mostly around my own age – young men who'd never fought in battle. In the year of the rebellion they would have been too young to fight, and since then, the Romans had enforced peace in our land.

As well as the youngsters, there were a few grey-headed men, and half a dozen women. (In my tribe there have always been women like Queen Boudicca - brave enough to go into battle.) My heart sank at the thought of this crowd coming face to face with a Roman legion. Against trained and disciplined soldiers, bravery wouldn't be enough.

Conan looked at me as if he could read my thoughts. "We're not alone," he said. "There are others gathering together, from the western Iceni and the Trinovantes. We're to meet at an island in the fen country. Then we march north through the lands of the Corieltauvi, gathering more men as we go. When we join up with the Brigantes, we will be a war host to be feared!"

"Do you really think we have a chance against the Romans?" I said.

"Of course we have a chance. And even if we lose the fight, at least we'll have struck a blow for our people. We'll have vengeance for our father, and all the others who died. That's only fair. The Romans killed them - the blood of Romans will pay for their death!"

Then there will never be an end to it, I wanted to say. We take revenge on them - they take revenge on us - on and on, for years and years, until there's no one left standing to fight.

But I said nothing. I knew he wouldn't understand.

***

It was dusk. The village was almost empty, for everyone had gone to the sacred grove in the forest.

Alain, the druid from Conan's army, was going to make a sacrifice to the gods.

Tiro, Felix and I stayed in the village, along with old Evan, who was too lame to walk so far. We sat outside the hut, as the sky darkened and stars appeared one by one. It was very peaceful – not a sound except for the murmur of the river.

"I wish you weren't going away," said Felix. "You could still change your mind."

"Conan would never forgive me," I said.

"Bryn, are you sure you're doing the right thing?" said Tiro.

"No. I'm not sure at all. Mother needs me for the harvest, and you need me as a translator... But Conan needs me, too."

"That's not what I meant. Is this right in God's sight, do you think – going out to war? We're meant to love our enemies, not fight them."

I cried out, "Love our enemies! Does that mean we just have to accept whatever they do to us? However cruel they are, however unjust, we simply have to let them get away with it?"

"I never said that. I don't believe—"

"Tiro, think of my people," I said. "The Romans are slowly killing what's left of them. As Christians, we're supposed to protect the widows and the fatherless, aren't we? The only way to do that is to attack the Romans and drive them out of our land."

"It's not the only way," said Felix. "There are better, more peaceful ways. We could go and see the procurator – persuade him to make the taxes less harsh."

"You try it," I said, grimly.

"I will. I'll try to speak with him when I go back to Londinium."

"And what makes you think he'll listen? He's a Roman, don't forget."

Felix said hotly, "So am I – don't forget. Not all Romans are greedy and cruel."

Tiro said, "Let's not argue. Especially not tonight, when we may never see each other again." In the darkness I couldn't see his face, but his voice was unbearably sad.

"You could always come with me, Tiro," I said. "You don't have any reason to love the Romans."

Tiro was silent for a moment. Then he said, "I can't, Bryn, because I don't think it's right, what you're doing. Think of Jesus – his people were conquered by the Romans, too. He could have led an army against them, and many people wanted him to. But that wasn't what he came to earth to do. He came to heal people and save them, not kill them."

I couldn't think of anything to say.

Tiro went on, "In any case, I think the rebellion will be useless. The Romans are too powerful. Even if an entire legion is destroyed, they'll simply call in more soldiers from Gaul or Germania. They've got the whole empire to back them up."

"So you think Britain is doomed," I said.

"Doomed? No. But I'd say it will be ruled by Rome for many years to come."

Felix said, "And that needn't be so terrible. Think of Gaul – think of southern Britain. The rule of Rome has been good for the people. They're peaceful and prosperous."

"Like slaves are peaceful and prosperous," I said, "as long as they obey. But I've had enough of being a slave."

A chill breeze blew up the valley. Gathering my cloak around my shoulders, I got up. It was time to make ready... time to go.

XIV

THE ISLAND

We set off in the middle of the night. There was a half moon, bright enough to light our path, without making us too visible from a distance.

"Where are we going?" I asked Conan.

"Westwards," was all he would say.

A young woman from the village had decided to come with us. Margaid was tall and slender, with hair the colour of a lion's mane. She was a widow – her husband had been killed in the great battle. She had no children, and little chance of marrying again, for all the young men were gone. (Except Conan, that is. I saw her eyes turn towards him now and then, but he hardly noticed her.)

"Why shouldn't I go to war?" she said. "My life is empty. I don't want to grow old without husband or children. Better to die in battle!"

"You're right," said Don. "Better to die in battle than go on living like this." I wondered if he was talking about the falling sickness. What would happen if he had another attack while we were on the march? Somehow I didn't think Conan would have much sympathy for him.

But at the moment he was fine. He looked excited, full of life. He was carrying one of the spears from my house; I had the other one. I gave the dagger to Margaid. She had no weapons of her own, unless you counted the small leather bag which went everywhere with her. I guessed what was in it – Margaid was the village expert on herbs and potions. Was she planning on poisoning the Romans one by one?

Conan already had weapons – a sword and a short throwing-spear. "Where did you get those?" I asked him. "They look Roman to me."

"That's because they are Roman. We ambushed a patrol last week. They never knew what hit them."

"You killed them all?" said Don, admiringly.

"Yes, and by the time their centurion started wondering why they didn't report back, we were long gone. Vanished like smoke!"

"Let's do it again," said Don. "We need more weapons."

Conan said, "Perhaps we will. Soon we'll have to cross a Roman road, and if the gods send a patrol into our hands..."

I really hoped that it wouldn't happen. More and more, I was wishing that I hadn't joined Conan's band.

The hunting spear that I carried was an old one. It had the marks of blood on its shaft – the blood of deer and wild boar. But soon I might have to use it against men. It would be stained with human blood.

Oh, God... I don't want to do this...

But God seemed a long way off. Tiro and Felix, too, were far distant, and I had no one to talk to; no one to help me pray.

I trudged on, my legs growing weary, my heart feeling heavier with each step I took. At last, Conan called a halt on the fringes of the forest. The sun, edging above the horizon, made long shadows over the flat, open land ahead. About half a mile away was a Roman road, a thin, straight line, like the scar of a sword cut.

"We'll spend the daylight hours here in the forest," said Conan. "Get some sleep, everyone. But I need two people to keep a look-out for anything moving on the road."

"I'll do it," said Don, eagerly.

"And me," I said, knowing Don wouldn't be much use as a lookout if the sickness came on him again.

All morning we lay hidden in the undergrowth at the forest's edge. Suddenly, Don nudged me. He pointed up the road. Far away to the east, I could just make out some movement.

"Is it a Roman patrol? Can we attack them?" he demanded.

I said, "Go and wake Conan."

By the time Conan arrived, crawling through the bracken, the moving figures had drawn closer. They were soldiers all right, dozens of them... No, more than that... two or three hundred, I estimated.

"We can't take on that lot," said Don, sounding disappointed.

I said, "They're heading westwards. Where do you think they're going, Conan?"

"Across the fens. The Romans have somehow managed to build a road through the marshes," said Conan. He couldn't quite keep the admiration out of his voice. "Then I suppose they'll turn northwards. The Roman general must be calling in troops from all over Britain."

For a while we gazed at the long column of marching men. Their armour glinted in the sunlight. They marched at the steady pace that would take them 20 miles in a day. They looked frightening – so strong, disciplined, and well armed. The line seemed to go on and on. Then, at last, it was past, dwindling into the distance.

Conan drew a long breath. "No need to mention this to the others," he said.

***

Another night of travelling brought us to the edge of the fen country – a vast marshland stretching to the west and north, further than I could see. Here and there were patches of solid ground, where stunted trees grew. Between them, dark brown streams moved sluggishly towards the sea. The warm breeze carried a smell of dampness and decay.

"Alain, you'll have to lead us now," said Conan, and the druid stepped forward.

"Stay close," he warned us. "It's easy to get lost out there."

It was daylight by now, but that didn't matter. There was no one to see us as we followed Alain deep into the marshland. We walked between banks of pale rushes higher than my head. Our path twisted and turned, sometimes doubling back on itself, sometimes crossing foul-smelling mud which sucked at our feet.

"Are we lost?" Don whispered after a time. "Where are we going?"

"I don't know. Conan said something about an island..."

We waded across a dark stream, where something nameless and slimy slithered against my legs. Huge blue dragonflies swooped and dived around us. The sun's heat was making the smell even worse; I decided I didn't like this place.

Then came a wider stretch of water, almost a lake. Alain came to a halt on the shore, and let out a high, piercing cry like the call of a bird.

A boat came gliding out of the reeds on the opposite bank. It was low and flat, designed for these shallow waters. The boatman used a long pole to propel it towards us.

Alain said, "The Romans don't know about this place, and they must never find out. Don't speak of it to anyone. If you do, may your tongue wither and your throat dry up! May those words be the last you ever speak!"

A few at a time, we were ferried across to the other side of the water. As I'd guessed, we had come to an island – quite a large one, encircled by alder trees. In the centre was an open space where sheep were grazing. There were several huts hidden in the trees on the opposite side.

"We must go and report to Prince Mark," said Conan.

"Who?"

"Our leader. He's a prince of the Corieltauvi tribe, from the far side of the fens. Most of his people are under Roman rule – they gave in without much of a fight. Not Mark, though!"

He led us towards the largest of the huts. "Wait here," Conan ordered, and he went inside.

I looked around the village. It was not unlike my own home, except for its hidden location. Probably the people were fishermen; there was a row of flat-bottomed boats pulled up on the shore. Many warriors were gathered here already, and among them I noticed several druids in their grey robes. They could wear them openly here without fear of the Romans.

After a time, Conan came out of the hut, followed by two armed bodyguards. Then came the man who must be the leader of this rag-tag army.

Prince Mark was quite young – not much older than Conan, I guessed. Tall and strong, he looked as if he would be a hard man in a fight. His sharp grey eyes examined us carefully. If he was disappointed in what he saw, he gave no hint of it.

"Welcome," he said. "We need every one of you. We need the wisdom of the old and the strength of the young, and the fierce courage of the women. In two days we'll set out through the lands of my people, and many more will join us. Then we'll meet with the warriors of the Brigantes. Together, we will face the Romans. Are you ready to fight?"

"We're ready!" came the roar, as we waved our spears – those of us who had them. "Death to all Romans!"

I saw why Conan was so keen to follow this leader into battle. I wanted to follow him too. He was a man who made you believe that anything was possible.

"Britain will be ours again," he cried. "We are going to drive the Romans into the sea! We'll fight a battle that the bards will sing about for years to come. Whether we live or die, our names will be remembered for ever!"

XV

BETWEEN THE
FIRES

The next day, two more bands of warriors arrived, one from the Trinovantes, the other from the western lands of my own people. There were now several hundred of us. Fortunately, some of the new arrivals had brought food supplies, for the villagers couldn't feed this number of people. They would probably be relieved when we went on our way, leaving them in peace.

In the afternoon, I noticed something going on at the far end of the island. The druids were busy there, collecting wood and building it into two heaps, close together. It reminded me of the bonfires we used to build on the eve of Beltane, the spring festival. We would drive the cattle between the two fires, asking the gods to give them many calves the following year.

"What's happening?" I asked Conan.

"You'll see later on."

"If it's for a sacrifice, I won't be there. You know I worship a different God now."

Conan looked angry for a moment, then he laughed. "What do you mean, you won't be there? Are you going to swim off the island?"

I hadn't thought of that. My heart sank.

"Anyway, you *have* to be there," said Conan. "You can only join the army if you walk between the two fires."

"That's not much of a test," said Don, scornfully. "In my tribe, you're not a warrior until you've killed a wolf or a wild boar, or brought back the head of an enemy."

"I don't think you'd find too many wolves on this island," I said. "Or enemies, either." But there I was wrong.

As night fell, the druids lit their fires. The flames looked very bright against the trees and the dark water. Everyone started moving towards them, and I went too. I didn't want to be seen as a stranger, an outsider. If Tiro or Felix had been there, I might have had the courage to be different from the crowd, but I couldn't do it alone.

We gathered together around the fires. Everyone fell silent. Then one of the druids prayed, asking Lugh, the sun god, to purify us with his fire.

"Let all fear be burned away. Send us out bravely, afraid of nothing, not even death. Give us the fire of your anger to make us great warriors, strong in battle!"

The flames gave a sudden leap as if in answer, making everyone gasp. I told myself there was nothing to fear. Probably a druid had thrown something on the fire to make it blaze like that. All the same, the hairs rose up on the back of my neck.

All my life, I'd been taught to worship these gods and fear them. Tiro said they didn't exist; but what if Tiro was wrong?

The old gods were fierce. They punished anyone who didn't respect and honour them. If you brought them gifts, they would be pleased with you for a time. They might help you. But they certainly didn't love you – not like the God I'd come to trust, the God who loved me as a father would.

I didn't want to go back to serving the old gods. And yet, in this place where they'd been worshipped for centuries, I felt the strength of their hold on me.

Help me, God! I want to follow you, only you. But I don't know if I'm strong enough. Help me!

I am with you always. I'll never leave you. You may be weak, but I am strong.

I heard the words as if they'd been spoken right in my ear. And suddenly I found the strength to walk away from the crowd. A few curious faces turned towards me, but no one said anything.

I went as far away as I could, which wasn't very far because of being on an island. The druid's voice sank to a murmur. Then came a sudden roar from the crowd. Something flew upwards, gleaming golden in the firelight, and fell into the smooth, black water. (Later, Don told me it was the gold neck ring that

Prince Mark had worn. He gave it as an offering to the gods, for victory in battle.)

The druids made everyone move to one side. It was time for people to walk between the two fires. I saw their shadowy figures, black against the flames. Don was right, I decided – it wasn't really a test of courage. To walk through the flames took only a few moments. Some men, trying to show off, stood still in the heat for as long as they could bear it, and one even danced a war dance, until his cloak caught fire. After that, people were more cautious.

Even from a distance, I recognised Don when it was his turn. He was one of the smallest and youngest, but he walked proudly towards the fire, his head held high. When he was between the fires, he stopped. At first I thought he was trying to show off, like the others. Then, quite slowly, his body crumpled to the ground.

Everyone gasped. A few people cried out. No one went to help him – instead the crowd drew back in fear.

The falling sickness! I ran towards him, hoping and praying that I wouldn't be too late. I saw that he had fallen in the narrow gap between the two fires. But he might still be badly burned.

"Help me get him away from the fire!" I cried.

No one moved. Don's body twitched and shook as I tried to drag him by the shoulders. He was too heavy for me. I would never do it on my own.

"Help me, somebody!"

The leader of the druids came closer. "Leave him," he ordered me. "The gods have marked him out. Leave him alone."

"No! It's only a sickness – it's happened before," I said. "We can't just leave him to burn!"

"Do you want to bring down the wrath of Lugh? Cheat the sun god of his chosen sacrifice?"

I stared at him, slowly realising what he meant. At Beltane, any animal which got singed by the fire was said to be chosen by Lugh. It would be sacrificed to him. But a human sacrifice! That was rare and terrible, only carried out at times of great need.

Times like this, on the eve of war...

"You're wrong," I said, feeling as if a deep pit had suddenly opened in front of me. "Lugh *didn't* choose him. He has an illness – the falling sickness." Desperately, I heaved at Don's shoulders, and managed to move him a little way. Oh God, help me!

"Stop him!" ordered the druid.

Three of the others tried to bar my way. But I knew they were afraid to come too close to Don while the strange fit was on him. With another great effort, I dragged him away from the fire. Just in time! His face was scarlet with heat, and his cloak was singed. He might be in pain – although at the moment he couldn't feel it – but at least he was alive.

"You have done wrong." The leader of the druids stared at me. He looked furious – he wasn't used to being disobeyed. "Now the gods will punish all of us."

"Sacrifice them both," said another druid.

"No!" cried Conan. But his voice was almost swallowed up by the yells of the crowd.

"Sacrifice them!"

"Give them up to Lugh!"

"Burn them!"

I stood up. "Burn me if you want to," I said, "but it won't win you any favour with Lugh. I serve a different God. When I die, I'll go to be with him."

It was quite amazing. I was filled with strength and courage which must have come from God. I didn't feel scared at all – not for myself. But then I looked at Don. What would they do to him?

"Don't kill Don," I pleaded. "You can see he's ill. Your gods don't like it if you sacrifice sick animals, do they? Only good ones – healthy ones."

Don had stopped his trembling and shaking. Now he was lying as if asleep. But the druids were still fearful of him, I could tell.

"The spirits have left him," one of them muttered. "But who knows when they'll come back?"

They drew aside and talked among themselves. The shouts of the crowd had died down to anxious muttering. I looked at the ring of faces, lit up by the firelight. Some were frightened, some angry, some grimly hostile. Even Conan looked as if he hated me.

"If you knew the kid had this... this illness," he hissed, "why didn't you tell me? I wouldn't have let him come with us."

"I'm sorry. I should have told you." But I'd been too busy trying to work out what I ought to do; I hadn't spared much thought for Don.

Prince Mark looked on silently. Although he was our leader, this was a matter for the druids to decide, here in their time of power. At last they made their minds up, and turned to face us.

"They are not to be burned," said the druid leader. "Lugh has rejected them. We won't kill the boy who is in the power of the spirits. That would only anger them, and they might take hold of someone else instead. We'll let the spirits deal with him, however they wish. Put him in a boat and set him adrift."

Nobody wanted to touch Don. But on the druids' orders, two men picked him up cautiously and carried him to the water's edge. They laid him in the bottom of a boat, then pushed it out from the shore. The slow current tugged at it; still unconscious, Don drifted off into the darkness.

"What about the other one?" someone shouted.

"He disobeyed us," said the druids' leader. "Worse, he disobeyed the gods. He has brought down their anger – let him bear it, then! Let him die the threefold death!"

XVI

THE DARK WATERS

I knew what the threefold death meant. Once before, long ago, I'd seen it happen. A man of my tribe was foolish enough to steal some gold offerings from a sacred well. The druids had him strangled, clubbed and stabbed, as if killing him three times over. Then they left his body in the marshes to rot.

At the thought of it, fear cut into me like a dagger. And I had a long time to think. While the rest of the warriors took their turn to walk through the flames, I was held prisoner, tied to a tree. Two druids watched me silently.

Oh, God... why are you letting this happen? Are the old gods stronger than you, after all? Help me – don't leave me!

There was no answer... no sound except the lapping of the dark waters.

Then I remembered another night of terror and darkness. On the deck of the ship, when I was afraid to jump into the sea, Tiro picked me up and threw me in. But he didn't leave me alone. He was there beside me. Even if I couldn't see him in the darkness, he was there helping me.

I had to trust that God was still there with me, in the darkness. I had to hope that, like Tiro, he knew what he was doing.

The ceremony finished at last. Then the druid leader turned towards me. He called out, "Untie him. Bring him here."

My guards, holding me by both arms, led me towards the fire. The crowd parted silently to let us through.

"Who brought this man here?" the leader demanded.

Conan stepped forward. "I did," he said, his voice harsh. "He's my brother, but I curse the day I asked him to join us!"

"Then you should strike the final blow. Take this dagger, and stand ready."

Conan was brought to stand in front of me. He couldn't look me in the face.

"Don't worry, Conan," I said, softly. "I'm going to meet with God. I'll live again after I die – live for ever!"

Still he wouldn't look at me, but stared at the ground. I saw how tightly he gripped the hilt of the dagger. He was a trained fighter; he knew how to use it. At least my death would be quick.

I heard an intake of breath from the crowd. The druids gripped my arms, as someone came up behind me on quiet feet. A cord was put around my neck, and slowly it began to tighten.

I choked. I couldn't breathe. Tighter and tighter the cord was wound. A red mist clouded my eyes, until I couldn't see anything except Conan's face.

I forgive you, brother, I wanted to say. But it was too late – I couldn't breathe or speak. I was about to die, and he would never know...

My legs gave way. I would have fallen, but the two druids held me upright. Then the noose seemed to slacken. But before I could gasp for breath, something smashed against my skull.

A lightning-flash of pain went right through me. And everything turned black.

***

Lap, lap... lap, lap... ripples licked my face like the tongue of an anxious dog. But they were cold, far colder than any living creature. Groaning, I tried to lift my head up, and felt a piercing stab of pain.

I was still alive, then. But how? And where was I?

Slowly I pieced things together. I was soaking wet – they must have thrown me in the river, thinking I was dead. But the cold water had revived me for a time. I dimly remembered struggling to keep my head above water, all the time knowing I mustn't make a sound. Keep floating, drift with the current... Oh, God, help me... Tired, so tired. Just let me sleep...

Now I was awake again. I had no idea how long I'd been lying here – wherever "here" was.

My throat was in agony when I tried to swallow. There was an ache deep in my side. Worst of all was the throbbing pain in my head, which made me feel dizzy. But at last I managed to sit up. I found myself on a mud bank, between the dark river and the murmuring reeds. Low in the sky hung a thin, pale moon.

Cautiously parting the reeds, I looked around. There was only darkness, and the glint of moonlight on water. Then, far in the distance, I saw the glow of a dying fire. That meant I was a good way from the island. For the moment I was safe.

Thank you, God! So you were with me all the time! You had your hand on me. You brought me out from the shadow of death...

Shivering, I managed to crawl through the reed beds to reach dry land. And there I sat, gathering my strength and waiting for daylight. Fortunately it was a warm, still night. My clothes slowly dried out on me, but I couldn't stop shivering. And my head... oh, my head...

I began to wonder how I could find my way out of the fens. The place was a tangle of winding streams, treacherous marshes, and paths which led nowhere.

You have to trust in God, I told myself. He's brought you this far, hasn't he?

As the huge, empty sky filled with the light of dawn, I struggled to my feet. Far upriver, I thought I could see the row of alder trees on the island. And downriver...

what was that low, dark shape? It almost looked like a boat - an empty boat.

I went closer. Yes, it was a boat, run aground in a loop of the river. But it wasn't empty.

"Don!" My voice was rasping, not like my own at all.

Don sat up, rubbing his eyes.

"What happened?" he asked, sleepily.

"Well..." I said, wondering where to begin.

Don said, "I was so scared. I must have had the sickness again, and when I woke up, everyone had disappeared. I was in this boat, all alone, gliding along in the dark..." Usually Don seemed old for his age, but now, suddenly, he looked very young. "I thought I was dead, or about to die."

"You weren't the only one," I said.

"I prayed to all the gods I could think of, but they didn't hear me. Then I remembered your God. I prayed to him, and then I fell asleep. Where are we?"

I told him all that had happened. His eyes widened.

"So you saved my life," he said.

"Yes, with God's help."

"You saved my life, and you almost got killed. Did Conan really stab you? Here, let me look."

The pain in my side had died to a dull ache. It flared up again as Don examined the wound.

"It doesn't look deep," he said. "He can't have been trying to kill you. I thought you said he's a trained fighter?"

"He is. But he's also my brother."

All at once I felt ridiculously happy. Perhaps Conan didn't hate me. Perhaps he'd tried to save me. After all, if he'd refused to use the dagger, someone else would have gladly taken it and finished me off.

Don was looking around, anxiously. "We ought to get out of here. But how? We don't know the paths through the marshes."

"Well, we've got a boat. All rivers find their way to the sea in the end, I suppose."

There was a pole lying in the bottom of the boat. I started trying to punt the boat along, but it wasn't an easy task. The end of the pole kept getting stuck in the mud; I almost lost it altogether. And I couldn't stand up for very long without feeling faint. My side ached. My head was still throbbing, as if a drummer was beating on my skull.

"Here, let me have a go," said Don. "You sit down and rest."

Gradually he got the hang of it. We slid downriver as the sun rose higher in the sky. In spite of the warmth, I couldn't stop shivering. I was feeling quite strange. When I looked at things in the distance, they seemed to swim hazily closer, then drift away again.

It was hard to know how far we'd travelled, because the river twisted and turned like a snake. And there were no landmarks in the fens.

"I'm starving," said Don. "How long before we reach the sea?"

"No idea. It might take days," I said.

"Maybe we should have gone up the river instead of down," said Don.

"Then we'd have had to pass the island. Not a good idea," I told him.

Soon after, we came to a place where our river joined another one. "Which way now? Upriver or down?" Don asked, steadying the boat.

"I don't know," I said, faintly. The sick, dizzy feeling was getting worse. "You decide."

Don gave me an anxious look. "Your face is as white as a shorn sheep. We ought to find someone who can help you, maybe clean that wound."

He gazed around, as if a town might suddenly appear out of the empty marsh. Then he pointed up river. I saw a thin thread of smoke rising, grey against the brilliant blue sky.

Don started punting the boat along with renewed strength. Even though the current was against us now, we were moving quite fast. "Slow down," I said. "We don't know if these people are friends or enemies."

A bend of the river brought us closer – not to a town or village, but to a solitary hut, small and low, thatched with reeds. A couple of goats were tethered close by. Don brought us inshore, just as someone came out of the hut. The man gave a startled cry.

All I noticed about him was his long, matted beard. "Oh, no! A druid!" I gasped. "Go back, Don!"

Too late. The boat had run itself aground. We were stuck.

XVII

NOT A HOPE

I needn't have been afraid. The stranger was not a druid. He was an ordinary man who lived alone and seldom met other people. So he didn't much care what he looked like. He hadn't shaved his beard in months. His face was brown and weathered, as if he spent most of his life outdoors.

When Don told him we needed help, he gave it, without asking questions. He cleaned up the wound in my side.

"It's only a flesh wound," he said. "It will heal, if you give it a day or two for the blood to thicken. That knock on the head looks bad, though. You ought to lie down and rest."

He offered me some water, but I couldn't drink it – my throat hurt too much. Then he let me lie down in the cool, shadowy hut. I drifted off into a sleep full of

terrifying dreams. Blazing fire... an angry druid...
Conan with a dagger in his hand...

When I awoke, it was evening. My head felt much
better; that throbbing pain was just a distant memory.
But when I tried to get up, I felt as weak as a reed stem.

"Bryn! You're awake!" Don sounded very relieved.
"How are you feeling? We were worried. You've been
ill for two days, and we couldn't get you to wake up."

"Two days..." I whispered.

"Here, let me get you a drink."

He brought me some goat's milk. Although my
throat still hurt, I found I could drink now, and eat a
little food. Gradually, I felt strength starting to come
back to me.

"Where's the man who helped us?" I asked Don,
after a while.

"Gareth? He's gone fishing," Don said. "He's a
strange kind of man. He was a warrior of the Iceni – he
fought in the great battle when Queen Boudicca was
defeated. Now he's had enough of fighting, he says."

Later, as we sat by the fire, Don asked Gareth what
it was like to fight in that battle. At first I didn't want to
listen, for it brought back memories of my father's
death. Staring into the hot, red heart of the fire, I tried
to shut out Gareth's voice. But I couldn't.

He told his story quietly. He didn't boast, or make
himself out to be a hero.

"The queen gave the word, and we charged up the
hill," he said. "But before we even reached the Roman
lines, a spear took her in the stomach. Then the Roman
soldiers threw another volley of spears. Charioteers

and horses were cut down, right in front of our foot soldiers as they came up the hill. After that, it was all just a mess.

"I got wounded in the shoulder, so I couldn't use my sword arm. I managed to crawl aside, to the edge of the forest. And I watched the Romans moving forward, all in line, like a great wave sweeping across a beach. Nothing could stop them.

"Then their cavalry came charging out from the woods on both sides. Our men were trapped between them. They were being pushed back down the hill, and I saw it was all over for us."

"So what did you do then?" Don asked.

"I ran away, of course – hero that I was." Gareth's voice was full of bitterness.

"What happened to Queen Boudicca?"

"Some people say she died of her wounds. Some say she took poison, so as not to be captured by the Romans."

"She was a great warrior," said Don, and he sighed. "If only she were alive now, to lead our people in battle again!"

"That wouldn't make any difference," said Gareth, wearily. "The Romans will defeat this new rebellion, just like the last one. They're like the tide coming in – you can stand in its path, but you can't stop it. In the end it will sweep you away."

I asked him why he chose to live this solitary life, out in the fens.

"At first I came here to hide, while my wounds healed," he said. "The Romans were hunting down everyone who had fought against them."

"But that was four years ago," I said. "Why don't you go back home, to the land of our people?"

"I did go back once, when I thought it was safe. It was a year after the battle. I found that the Romans were building a fort where my village had been. They were crushing the life out of my people with their taxes and laws. What was there to go home for?"

I felt disappointed. Gareth was a warrior. He'd seen how cruelly our people were treated, but he had just walked away. He'd given up hope of ever changing things.

It was better to fight! Then I remembered... that road was closed to me. I couldn't rejoin Prince Mark's army. But on my own, I was powerless to change anything. I too was giving up, walking away.

Dimly, I remembered something Felix had said. "There are better, more peaceful ways." What did that mean?

But Don was talking again, asking how we could find our way out of the fens. Gareth described the Roman causeway, a day's journey upriver. Eastwards, it led towards the lands of my people. Westwards, it joined the great Roman road running up the spine of Britain.

"Where are you going?" he asked us.

"Back to my village," I said. "What about you, Don? Do you still want to go back to your own people?"

"I'll go wherever you go," he said. "I would be dead if it wasn't for you. My life belongs to you now. Maybe one day I can repay you by saving *your* life."

I was taken aback. "But Don, you don't owe me anything. You already helped to save me from the pirates."

He shook his head. "That was for my sake, not yours – to help me escape. What you did was different. You put your own life in danger to save mine. So now I'll follow you and be your shield-bearer. That's the custom of my tribe."

"I don't need a shield-bearer," I protested. "I don't even have a shield."

"Don't you want me to come with you?" he said, looking hurt.

"It isn't that. Come home with me – stay as long as you like. But I know what it's like to feel homesick for your own tribe and birthplace. If that happens, you must be free to go back to your people."

"No," said Don. "I thought I could go back home and prove myself as a warrior. But the queen was right – what use is a fighter who falls down before the battle? Among my people, if you're not a warrior, you're worthless. They would despise me and laugh at me, just as they always did."

"Don, you're not worthless," I said. "You're as brave as any warrior I've ever known."

But he wasn't listening. "Anyway, all the people I loved are dead," he said. And echoing Gareth's words, he added, "What is there to go home for?"

***

A couple of days later, I felt strong enough to travel. We said goodbye to Gareth, thanking him for all his help. Then we got in the boat and set off upriver. It was a long, slow journey. A heat haze hung over the water; fish rose lazily for flies. The ripples of our wake made the reeds tremble as we glided past.

I was thinking about what Don had said about the custom of his tribe. When we stopped for a rest, I asked him about it.

"If someone saves you from death, that means your life belongs to him - is that right?"

"Only if it cost him dearly... if he put himself in danger, or got wounded in battle, to save you."

"There is someone who did far more for you than that. He actually died for your sake." And I talked about the death of Jesus, God's Son. It wasn't the first time Don had heard this - Tiro had told the story before. But Tiro hadn't known about this tribal custom. It helped me to explain things.

"Jesus died, and took the punishment for all the wrong things I've ever done. He saved me. His death means I'll live for ever. So I gave my life to him - I belong to him. And you can do that too, if you want to."

Don said, "Yes. I want to follow him. I want your God to be my God too."

He said it so easily, I wasn't sure he really understood.

"What must I do?" he asked. "How do I become a follower of your God?"

"You pray to him, saying you're sorry for the bad things in your past life. Tell him you want to give your life to him from now on."

"All right," said Don. He prayed, then looked at me, as if he expected something else to happen.

"And then you should be baptised – that means going under water and coming up again. It's like a sign that you've gone from the old life to the new one. But perhaps not here," I said, looking at the shallow, muddy river. "We can do that when we get home."

Don looked relieved.

"So that's all? Now I belong to God?" he said.

"Yes." I really hoped he meant what he said, and wasn't just doing this to please me. But that was for God to judge, not me.

"We'd better get going, then," Don said, and pushed the boat out into the stream.

***

As time went on, we saw that the river was getting narrower. Now and then our boat grounded in the shallow water. "Where's this road Gareth mentioned?" Don kept asking.

And then we saw it ahead of us, flat and level as the horizon. It was an impressive sight. A gravel causeway had been built across the marshy ground, with a bridge over the river. Unlike the crooked paths and winding streams of the fens, the Roman road was as straight as a stretched bowstring.

We abandoned the boat at the riverside. As we reached the road, an ox cart was approaching, heading eastwards. I glanced at the driver, then at the man who was riding in the cart. Hey, that face looked familiar...

"Costicos!" I cried. I hadn't seen him since the quayside at Portus Ardaoni. "How's the wine trade these days?"

"Oh, fine, fine," he said, looking blank. I could tell he hadn't a clue who I was. But then, last time we met I was in Roman clothes, with shorter hair, and no bloodstains on my tunic.

He looked at Don, then back at me, and then he remembered.

"Bryn! How are you doing? You look much more, er... *British* than you used to."

He told the driver to stop, and we talked for a while. He still had a few amphorae of wine in the cart – the last of his cargo. All the rest had been sold (very profitably, he boasted). He'd been travelling through the Corieltauvi lands, but there were rumours of a rebellion.

"This morning I called at an army post," he said, "and the soldiers advised me to get out of the area. It's going to be a battlefield in a few days."

"From what I heard, the real trouble will be further north," I said, "among the Brigantes."

"Ha! That's what everyone thinks, but they're wrong. The rebel Brigantes were defeated two days ago... utterly crushed. Their ex-king, Venutius, or whatever his name is, escaped alive. But it will be a while before he can persuade anyone to fight for him again."

"How do you know this?" Don demanded.

"An army messenger stopped at the post to change horses – that's how I know. He was heading for Londinium with the news. The Roman general is preparing to march south to take on the rest of the rebels."

My heart sank like a stone. Prince Mark and his men had been hoping to fight alongside the Brigantes. But that would never happen now. They would have to stand alone against the might of the Roman army.

"When will these foolish tribesmen learn that it's useless to rise up against Rome?" said Costicos. "They haven't a chance. Not a hope."

XVIII

THE FORT

There was only one thought in my mind – warn Conan.

"Are you heading eastwards?" Costicos asked me. "You can ride with me if you want."

"Thanks, but I'm going the opposite way," I said. "I have to find my brother."

"Very well. I wish you a safe journey!" he said. "Drive on."

Don was very quiet as we walked along the road. I thought it was because of the bad news about Venutius' army. "Utterly crushed," Costicos had said, and Don knew what the Romans did to their defeated enemies.

After a time he said, "It was a chance in a thousand that we met Costicos like that, and heard the news."

"Not chance," I said. "It was God's will."

"So you think God is telling you to warn your brother and his friends?"

I nodded.

He said, "You do know they won't exactly be pleased to see you again, don't you?"

"That's a risk I have to take," I said. "God saved me before, and he can do it again. You needn't take the risk, though, Don."

His face took on that stubborn look. He said, "I'll go wherever you go."

We trudged on along the endless-looking causeway. The sun was setting over the fens, turning the pools and streams blood red. I was starting to feel weary, and my side ached with each step I took.

Don said, "We may be too late with our warning. How long have we got before the Romans appear?"

"There should still be time," I said, for I'd been thinking about this. "The Roman legions travel on foot, not nearly as fast as a messenger on horseback. It could take them several days to march south."

"Yes, but it might take us days to catch up with our army. We don't even know where they are."

As night was falling, we came to a village on the edge of the fens. (Oh, it felt good to get away from that hard, straight road.) The people belonged to the Corieltauvi tribe. They were friendly enough, until we mentioned Prince Mark and his army.

It seemed that not everyone supported the prince.

"He's a young fool," said one of the men. "He'll bring down trouble on all of us. If the Romans defeat him, they'll punish the whole tribe. Look what happened to the Iceni."

"And why should we join forces with the Brigantes?" said another. "They've always been our enemies. Whenever they have a lean winter, they attack our borders and steal our sheep. At least the Romans protect us from them."

This made Don clench his fists, but he said nothing.

"I heard the Romans had defeated King Venutius and his Brigantes," I said. "Do you know if it's true?"

The man shrugged. "It takes months for news to reach us from the north."

"Where is Prince Mark gathering his army?" Don asked.

"At Deer Hill, on the northern borders of our land," the first man said. "Are you planning to join them? You're crazy."

But at least they gave us a bed for the night and some food in the morning.

For two days we travelled through the land of the Corieltauvi. On our way, we crossed a Roman road which seemed to mark some kind of boundary. The land beyond hadn't yet been taken over by the Romans. The people were free to live as they had always done, paying no taxes to Rome. They still belonged to the same tribe, but seemed more warlike than the others we'd met. Many of their men had gone to join Prince Mark.

His warriors were still gathering at Deer Hill, we heard. Soon they would be marching north.

"Do you think the Romans know about them?" I asked a woman, when we stopped to ask the way.

"They know, all right. They have their spies. Two of them were here yesterday, snooping around, asking where to find the rebel army. If my man had been here, he'd have taught them a lesson!"

"Spies?" said Don. "How did you know they were spies?"

She laughed. "One was a young Roman who couldn't even speak our language. The other was a big man with a face as black as charcoal. They didn't exactly look as if they belonged here! Don't worry, we didn't tell them anything."

As we went on, Don said what I'd been thinking. "Strange. That sounded just like Felix and Tiro."

"It couldn't be," I said. "What would they be doing here?"

"Looking for us?"

It was a frightening thought. But surely Tiro would never let Felix venture out here, where Romans were the enemy... where there were no soldiers to enforce the peace of Rome.

"They wouldn't do anything so risky," I said. "Felix might want to, but Tiro would have more sense. They're probably still at my village, helping to get the harvest in."

I prayed that it was true.

***

The land was becoming rougher and steeper. The valleys were green, the swelling hills brown with heather. "This is better than that stinking marsh," said Don. "It's more like the land of my birth."

The place called Deer Hill turned out to be a hill fort. We saw it on the skyline, from a long way down the valley. A zigzag path took us up to the outer defence – a steep earth bank surrounding the hilltop. Then came a dry ditch and an inner wall of earth and stones, topped with a wooden fence. There were heavy gates standing open, for it was daylight, with no enemy in sight. (Up here, enemies would be visible when they were still miles away.)

"Come to join us, have you?" asked one of the guards at the gates.

"I'm looking for my brother," I said, and he let us pass.

Beyond the gates, there was a large, open space, dotted with roughly built huts and shelters. In times of danger, it would be big enough to hold the people of several villages, along with their sheep and cattle. But now it was filled with Prince Mark's warriors. The army seemed to have grown quite a lot, and gained a good number of horses – even a few war chariots.

We wandered up and down, looking for Conan. At first we didn't see anyone we knew – then I spotted Margaid. She was beside a cooking fire, stirring oatmeal into a pot.

"Hey, Margaid! You don't know where Conan is, do you?" I called.

She looked up, and her face went white. "Bryn!" she gasped. "Don't come near me! I never did you any harm, I swear it!"

Of course – she believed I was dead. She'd seen me being killed three times over. She thought she was looking at a spirit walking in broad daylight.

"It's all right. Look, I'm still alive! They didn't manage to kill me," I said. "And they didn't get rid of Don, either."

She looked at Don, then back at me. Very slowly, she put out a hand and touched me, as if to make sure I was real.

"I can't believe it," she whispered. "How can you still be alive?"

"God took care of me," I said, "with a bit of help from Conan."

Margaid's face showed a mixture of wonder and fear. "Wait till Conan sees you! He thinks you're dead, and it's all his fault. He keeps saying he should have made you stay at home."

"Where is he?" I demanded.

"He rode out yesterday with Prince Mark, trying to gather more warriors. The prince chose him to be one of his bodyguards. Everyone says it's a great honour," she said. Something in her voice told me she might not agree.

"Do you know when they'll come back?" Don asked.

"Tonight or tomorrow. Or maybe the next day."

Oh, no... The Romans must be marching closer each day. How much time did we have left?

Suddenly I was aware of a commotion behind us. A crowd was gathering near the gates of the fort. I heard angry shouts.

"Kill them!"

"Roman spies! How did they find us?"

"Kill them! Kill them!"

People ran to join the crowd, trying to find out what was going on. It was impossible to see who or what was at the centre of the group. The confused mass of warriors moved closer to us. Unlike in the Roman army, there was no one to take charge, no one giving orders.

Someone shouted, "Don't kill them. Take them to Prince Mark first."

"He's not here. Get rid of them! Roman pigs!"

"They deserve to die!"

Through the shouting, I heard a voice I knew very well, struggling to speak the Celtic language.

"Don't kill us until you've heard what we have to say! Listen, will you?"

"Tiro!" I breathed. "And Felix! What did they come here for?"

"They must be mad," Don whispered. "They won't get out alive."

XIX

GOOD NEWS, BAD NEWS

I ran towards the crowd of warriors, with Don close behind me. It seemed impossible to get anywhere near the centre of the group. But then, as I pushed and shoved, a few people near me realised who I was. Terrified, they drew back from me as if I could destroy them with a single glance.

I heard shocked whispers running through the crowd.

"That's Conan's brother – the one the druids killed."

"Don't be stupid. It can't be him."

"It is him, I'm telling you! Or his ghost..."

Many of them hadn't even been there, that night on the island. But they were affected by the panic of those who had. People fought to get away from me. A gap

opened up in the crowd, and I stepped into the centre
of the circle.

"Bryn!" Felix gasped. "Tell them we don't mean any
harm!"

He stood back to back with Tiro, surrounded by
armed warriors. Felix looked very frightened. Tiro
seemed calmer, but there was sweat on his brow.

"It's all right," I said to the warriors around them.
"These men aren't spies."

"Then what are they doing here?" said one man,
jabbing his spear towards Felix. I recognised him as the
guard who'd let us in. "This isn't Roman territory. But
they marched up here as if they owned the place."

"Just arrived at the gate, in broad daylight?" said
Don. "Useless spies, if you ask me."

The crowd was quiet now, except for the odd
whispers I could just hear. Yes, that's him all right...
threefold death... the druids...

"Why did you come here?" I asked Tiro.

"Because we've got good news. There's a new
procurator in charge of tax in Britain. He thinks it's
wrong to keep punishing the tribes for the last
rebellion, making them pay such heavy taxes. From
now on, the Iceni and the Trinovantes will only have to
pay half as much tax."

I stared at him. "How do you know?"

"We spoke to the man himself!" said Felix. "It was
my idea. We would have gone all the way to
Londinium, but we didn't need to. He was at
Camulodunum, starting out on a tour of the country.
We asked to speak to him. We told him what things are

like in the villages – how desperate the people are, and how they hate Rome, all because of the tax collectors."

Tiro said, "He's a fair-minded man. Even before we met him, he'd started to think that the taxes should be lowered. It's really going to happen, Bryn! Tell your people. If they know about this, they may not go to war."

"Taxes aren't the only reason people go to war," I said, doubtfully. "Half of these people have never paid tax in their lives, but they still want to get rid of the Romans."

By now, some of the warriors were growing restless. They didn't like us speaking in Latin.

"What's he saying?"

"They're all spies. Kill the lot of them!"

"How are you going to kill the one who's already dead?"

I turned to the crowd. "I am not a ghost," I said. "It's true I'm the one the druids tried to kill, but they didn't succeed. I serve a God who's more powerful even than Lugh – that's why I am alive."

Through the crowd I saw Alain, the druid, looking furious. I'd better beware. He might try to succeed where his friends had failed.

"And these men," I went on, "are not Roman spies. They've brought a message that everyone should listen to." Quickly I translated what Tiro had said. But it didn't have the effect he had hoped.

"Taxes halved – what's so great about that?" someone shouted. "Why should we pay any taxes at all?"

"When we get rid of the Romans, we won't have to!" yelled someone else.

"Death to the Romans!"

This was all going wrong. It felt as if we were balanced on a cliff-edge. If a single warrior used his spear in earnest, then the whole crowd would join in, stabbing, shouting, and trampling us underfoot.

Suddenly I heard hoof-beats. A group of horsemen rode in through the gateway of the fort, with Prince Mark in the lead. Craning my neck, I spotted Conan towards the rear of the group.

"Where are the guards who should be at the gates?" Prince Mark shouted, reining in his horse. "We could have been enemies riding in, with no one to stop us!"

I thought, if he expects obedience and discipline, he's with the wrong army. He ought to join the Romans.

Prince Mark rode towards us. "What's going on?" he asked, and a dozen men tried to tell him all at once.

"Roman spies? Bring them here."

Along with Felix and Tiro, Don and I were hustled forwards through the crowd. When Mark saw me, his eyes widened in sudden fear, and his hand went to his sword-hilt.

"Bryn!" Conan had seen me too. He leapt from his horse and ran towards me. "Oh, Bryn, I can't believe it. I was sure you were dead!"

"No. I'm still alive – thanks to you."

"Are you all right?"

"Not bad, except that somebody tried to stab me the other day." I grinned at him. "Didn't make a very good job of it, though."

Then the smile left my face. Alain, with his hate-filled eyes, was standing quite close to us. He must have heard every word.

Lowering his voice, Conan said, "You shouldn't have come here. It's far too dangerous."

"I had to come – I had to make sure you heard the news." I took a deep breath. "The Romans have defeated King Venutius of the Brigantes."

"What did you say?" Prince Mark demanded.

I turned to face him. "Four days ago, the Romans defeated King Venutius. And now they're marching south to attack you. They must be well on the way by now."

He stared down at me from the saddle of his horse. "I've heard nothing of this," he said, coldly. "How could you possibly hear such news? Only an eagle could carry the word so swiftly from the northern hills."

"An eagle, or a Roman messenger," I said. I explained how the news had reached me.

"That's nothing but a rumour," the prince said angrily, and his horse took a nervous side-step. "I don't believe a word of it! And I won't, unless I see for myself the smoke of the Roman campfires. I don't see any reason to change our plans."

"This is madness," I said. "You can't fight the Romans unaided."

"More warriors are gathering to our banner every day!" cried Prince Mark. He drew his sword and held it aloft. "Soon we'll have an army to put fear into the hearts of even the Romans! We march north in three days. Are you with me?"

"Yes!" roared the crowd.

As their voices died down, Don shouted, "You're all mad. You'll be marching to your deaths!"

"Don't listen to that boy," Alain cried out. "He's in the power of evil spirits. Don't listen to his lies! We should kill him now, before the spirits take hold of him again."

"No. At least, not yet," said Prince Mark. He hesitated, and for a moment I saw fear in his eyes. But he was the leader; he had to appear strong and in control.

"Put these four under guard," he ordered. "Yes – the Romans too. Make sure no one goes near them. I'll deal with them later."

We were taken to an empty hut. It had no door, but a group of spearmen stood guard at the entrance. They watched us suspiciously as we talked together, telling all that had happened since we saw each other last.

"What now?" asked Felix. "What will they do to us?"

"I don't know," I said, feeling helpless. "Why didn't Prince Mark believe me?"

"He didn't *want* to believe you," said Tiro. "He's managed to persuade his warriors that they are strong enough to take on the Romans. He can't bring himself to say, 'Sorry, I was wrong. We don't have a chance – everyone go home.'"

Felix said, "Because he would look a fool, you mean? But he'll look even more of a fool when his followers are massacred by the legions."

"No," I said, "he'll be a hero. My people love dead heroes. The bards will write songs about the last ride of Prince Mark, bravest of the Corieltauvi... Look at Queen Boudicca. I bet she'll still be famous in a hundred years, even though she caused the ruin of my tribe."

The daylight was fading. Still no orders came from Prince Mark. Perhaps he'd forgotten we existed. Perhaps he was discussing us with his trusted men... or with the druids.

I remembered the hatred I'd seen in Alain's eyes, and shivered. Probably Conan, having failed to kill me, was in danger too. But there was nothing I could do about it.

Tiro said, "How long before the Romans arrive? If Prince Mark's still here then, this fort will turn into a trap he can't escape from."

Tiro was right. I knew the fort had been built for defence against raiding tribesmen, not Roman legions. If Prince Mark tried to use it as a refuge, the Romans would knock holes in the barrier with a ballista, or simply encircle the fort and starve the defenders out.

"We'll probably be dead before then," Felix said, grimly. "We have to get out of here!"

He got up and paced restlessly around the hut. I saw what he was doing – looking for any weak place in the walls. But the guards noticed too. They forced him back to us at spear point and made him sit down.

Don nudged me. "We should pray to God. Like you said, he saved us before and he can do it again."

So we prayed together under the watchful eyes of the guards, as night fell, and shadows crowded in on us.

XX

OVER THE WALL

"I've brought you some food."

Don and I looked up hopefully. But the woman who stood outside, hooded in her cloak, was talking to the guards, not to us. She handed them a pot of stew and some bread.

"Hey, what about us?" Don protested. But the woman didn't answer, just hurried away.

We hadn't eaten since breakfast time. Our mouths watered at the smell of food, as the guards sat down by the doorway to eat. We watched them like hungry dogs, eyeing every move they made. But they didn't leave us a single mouthful.

It was quite dark now. The hut, with no fire at its centre, was a chilly place. We wrapped ourselves in our cloaks and lay down on the hard earth floor, trying to get comfortable enough to sleep. Our guards, too, were starting to yawn.

"Why don't we take it in turns to get some rest?" one of them suggested. "It doesn't need six of us to guard that lot."

Three of them lay down. The other three, armed with their spears, sat silently in the doorway. From outside came the sounds of the camp settling down for the night: the neigh of a horse, the murmur of voices, a sudden burst of laughter.

Then I heard something else... the sound of snoring near the door.

Felix crept towards the guards, then came back to us. "Would you believe it?" he whispered. "They've all gone to sleep!"

"What? The whole lot of them?"

"The food must have been drugged," said Tiro. "But who could have done that?"

Margaid, I thought at once.

"Never mind who did it," muttered Felix. "Let's go! Let's get out of here!"

"No, wait," Tiro whispered. "We still have to find our way out of the fort. Will the gates be shut by now?"

"We'll have to go over the walls," I said.

Tiro said, "Then we should wait until—"

Suddenly he fell silent. Someone was standing in the doorway.

"Well?" Conan said, softly. "Anyone awake in there?"

"Only us," I said.

"Come out, then. Quick! We haven't much time."

The most frightening moment was when we had to step over the sleeping guards in the doorway. One of them stirred and grunted something. I thought my heart would stop. But somehow we all got out safely.

"Keep down," whispered Conan.

Here and there, a few cooking fires still flickered, but this made the darkness between them seem even darker. We crept from the shadow of our hut to another one, closer to the boundary wall and fence. As I reached it, a hand touched my arm. I almost cried out.

"It's me, Margaid. I want to go with you," she whispered.

Conan told us, "The fence isn't too high on this side. On the other side, there's a steep drop into the ditch. Be ready for it. Don't make a sound! There's a lookout further along, but I'm going to talk to him. Wait until I get there."

"But Conan, aren't you coming too?" I whispered urgently. "When they find we're gone, Alain will blame you straight away. They'll kill you!"

"I'll come if I can, but don't wait for me. Just get away from here." And he disappeared into the shadows.

The sky was clear, the stars very bright. Fortunately, the thin fingernail of moon didn't give much light. Dark against the stars, I saw the top of the fence, and the lookout man along to the right. Then Conan appeared beside him.

"Come on," whispered Felix.

We darted towards the shelter of the fence. A moment's pause... but everything was quiet. No one had seen us.

I prepared myself to make the climb and the jump. This was as frightening as that leap from the ship into the sea. But God was with us then, and he was still with us. I held onto that thought like a weapon.

Tiro helped Margaid up. Keeping low to the top of the fence, she scrambled over. There was a muffled thud from the other side as she hit the ground.

The rest of us went over one by one. With a silent prayer, I gripped the top of the fence and swung myself over. I rolled down into the shadows of the dry ditch between the inner and outer defences.

The outer defence was just a bank of earth. It would be easy for us to climb – and easy for the lookout to see us.

"What's on the other side?" whispered Tiro.

I tried to remember what I'd seen on the way into the fort. "A steep slope down. It's quite open at first. Lower down, gorse bushes and bracken."

"The lookout will spot us," muttered Don. "Unless he's totally blind."

Suddenly I heard Conan's voice. He sounded startled. "What's that down there? Did you see it?"

I froze. Just for a moment, I thought Conan had betrayed us. Had he helped us escape, only to have us captured again?

"Where?" cried the guard.

"Look, over there, on the right."

It was all right. He was pointing away from us, distracting the lookout's attention.

"Let's go," whispered Tiro. "Keep down and to the left."

We scrambled over the outer wall, hearing Conan argue with the lookout.

"I can't see anything," the lookout was saying.

"Well, I definitely saw something move. Keep your eye on that white rock – look, over there."

"Probably a fox or a hare," the lookout said.

"No, it was too big for that."

"What did it look like then – a Roman?" the man said, mockingly. "Maybe a whole legion of Romans? Don't panic. The only Romans near here are those two fools we captured earlier."

Their voices faded as we scurried down the hill and dived into the shelter of the gorse bushes.

"Is everyone here?" Tiro asked.

"Everyone except Conan," I said. "How's he going to get out?"

No one answered.

***

We went cautiously down the hill, keeping under cover. As we approached the track along the valley bottom, we tried to decide which way to go.

"East, down the valley," said Felix. "That's the quickest way back to civilis... I mean, to safety."

Don understood his words. "Safety for *him*," he said.

"Safety for all of us," said Tiro. "Prince Mark's warriors think we're spies. They won't want us to tell the Romans what we know. They'll be after us as soon as they find we've escaped."

"Maybe we should go up the valley, then," I said. "They won't expect that."

Just then we heard the sound of hoof-beats on the path leading down from the fort.

"Quick! Hide!" Felix hissed. But before we could retreat into the bracken, I saw that there was no need. There was only one rider, and it was Conan.

"However did you get out?" I asked.

"Easy! Through the main gates. The men on guard knew me. They unbarred the gates when I told them I was on a mission for Prince Mark."

I wanted to laugh out loud.

Conan said, "Listen – we don't have much time. When I left, the prince was with his counsellors, trying to decide what to do. Any time now, they could discover you're missing."

"Which way should we go?" I asked.

"East, of course." He sounded surprised. "I don't know about you, but Margaid and I are going home."

We set off down the valley, all the time looking for possible hiding places if we were pursued – a forest or a fern-covered hill. We passed a couple of villages, but it was late and all the doors were shut. No one saw us.

On and on we walked. When Margaid's feet grew tired, Conan dismounted and put her on his horse. The valley began to open out onto a plain. But it was almost dawn, and we were still a long way from the

Roman road which would mean safety. The warriors wouldn't dare to hunt us down in Roman-held territory.

When we reached some dense woodland, Conan said, "Better hide here until dark. I'll ride on for a mile or two, in case they follow the tracks of the horse. Then I'll double back to you."

Conan seemed to have become the leader of our party. Obeying orders, we slipped between the trees, trying to leave no signs that a hunter might notice. Secretly, I thought he was being too cautious. After all, there had been no sign so far of anyone following us.

We chose a place to lie in the bracken, well back from the track. As the first sunlight came slanting through the trees, I began to drift off to sleep. But then a noise jerked me awake again.

Horses! A good number of them, by the sound of it. Ten? Fifteen?

"Over here!" someone shouted. "See – the trail's still fresh. They can't be far ahead."

Margaid gave a little gasp, and I saw that she was as worried as I was. For Conan had still not returned.

The men rode on. We lay there, silently listening. The sounds of the hunt faded into the distance. Then there was nothing to hear except birdsong and whispering trees.

XXI

HARVEST

After a time, when there was still no sign of Conan, I grew too anxious to wait any longer. Cautiously, I crawled through the undergrowth towards the edge of the woodland. Then I heard the sound of hooves again, like the frantic beat of a drum. A band of horsemen went past at a gallop.

They were heading back the way we had come, up the valley. Were they the hunters who had been on our trail? Had they managed to capture Conan? But their furious pace didn't look to me like a ride of triumph – more like terror.

I gazed after them until they disappeared round a twist of the track. Then I saw a lone rider coming along the edge of the wood. Conan!

I ran out to meet him. "What happened?"

"They saw the Romans. That's what happened," said Conan, grimly.

"The Romans!"

"Yes. They're only a few miles away – you can see them from that ridge. There's a huge encampment on the plain. They must outnumber us ten to one."

"Maybe Prince Mark will believe me now," I said.

Conan said, "Prince Mark's a fool. I wouldn't be surprised if he tried to defend the fort, even though he's only got enough food supplies for a few days. A glorious defeat that the bards will sing about for a thousand years!" His voice was savage.

"What do you think he should do?" I asked.

"Disband his army, of course – send everyone home. Let them live to fight again some other time. They could all get away into the hills before the Romans reach the fort. As for Mark himself, I suppose there'll be a reward for his capture. He ought to escape into the mountains of the far west, where people are still free. I hope he has enough sense to do it."

By now the others, hearing our voices, had come to join us. Don said, "You sound as if you don't think much of Mark as a leader."

"I used to believe everything he said. Not any more," Conan said. "It's true he's good at getting people to follow him, but that doesn't make him a good leader. He's hopeless at deciding what to do. We could have marched north days ago."

Margaid said, "And we could have all been killed by now. It's no use thinking about what might have happened."

But Conan was gazing up the valley, as if part of him longed to be back at the fort, preparing to fight.

"Come on, Conan," I said. "We don't want to be here when the Romans arrive."

Don said, "And you'd better not be caught with *that*." He pointed to the stolen Roman sword which Conan wore.

"Yes, you're right." With a sigh, he undid his belt, took off the sword and scabbard, and let them fall to the ground. He flung his spear far into the woods.

"Let's go home," he said.

***

It was days before we found out what had happened to Prince Mark's army.

We were back at home, getting in the last of the harvest. As evening fell, two men – one young, one old – came trudging wearily down the valley. Conan recognised them at once. They had been members of his warrior troop.

"What happened? Was there a battle?" he demanded.

The old man shook his head. "Prince Mark said we couldn't fight the Romans. Their army was too big. We would have been totally outnumbered."

"Well, I still think we should have fought them," the young man said, angrily. "Instead, we crept away like cowards – like beaten dogs. They must have laughed at us!"

"So Prince Mark disbanded the army?" I said.

"Yes," said the old man. "We scattered in all directions. When the Romans arrived, there would be nothing for them to find except the empty fort. Prince Mark himself was long gone. I've heard he rode towards the west, heading for the mountains."

"That was a wise choice," said Conan.

The young man said, "He promised he would return one day, at the head of a great army."

"Would you fight for him again?" Don asked.

"I'll fight for anyone who will lead us against the Romans!" said the young man.

The old man shook his head. "Prince Mark is better at talking than fighting," he said. "I wouldn't follow him again. As for his great army, I'll believe it when I see it."

That reminded me of something that the prince had said. He'd refused to believe me when I warned him that the Romans were coming. What had made him change his mind?

When I asked the old man, he said, "Some horsemen brought the news that they'd actually seen the Roman camp, spread out over the plain. They'd never seen so many Romans all in one place. And they were terrified – you could see it in their faces. Only a fool would doubt their words."

Don said to me, "Maybe Gareth was right. The Romans are like the incoming tide – you can't stop them."

"In the end, every tide must turn," the old man said. "It may not be in our time, or our children's time... but one day our land will be free again."

We invited them to spend the night in our village. But their own home wasn't far away, and they were keen to get back there.

As they turned to go, the young man said to Conan, "You know, you would make a better leader than Prince Mark. I'd follow you into battle any day."

"Not me," said Conan. "For now, I'm going to listen to my mother's advice. Find a wife and settle down."

"Margaid would make a good wife, I think," the young man said.

"Well, you can't have her," said Conan, smiling. "I saw her first."

***

After the harvest was gathered in, Felix began to plan his journey back to Gaul. Tiro, Don and I would go with him part of the way, as far as the south coast of Britain, to help him transport the cloth we'd bought. It should fetch a good price in southern Gaul. Even allowing for what the tax collector had taken, Felix thought he would still be able to repay Septimus the money we had borrowed.

"And next summer, if God wills, I'll make another trip," he said. "Perhaps Septimus will come too. We'll do some trading, and come to visit you."

"But I thought you hated Britain," I said. "A half-civilised mud-hole, you called it."

"Well, I was wrong. It isn't even half-civilised," he said, grinning.

"I bet he never comes back here," Don said to me in our own language.

"I might surprise you one day," Felix said to him in Latin, and we gaped at him. He'd understood Don's words!

"It's amazing what you can pick up without even trying," said Felix. "Like fleas. Oh, I can't wait to get back to a decent-sized town, with baths and toilets and proper food."

"Won't you miss that kind of thing, Tiro?" I asked.

"Maybe a little. What I'll miss most is the heat of the sun." The wind made him shiver slightly; autumn was nearly here. I wondered how Tiro would feel in the depths of our winter.

For Tiro had decided not to return to Gaul with Felix. He was sure that God wanted him to stay in Britain, where no one had heard the good news of Jesus. It was possible to speak freely here without being arrested... unlike Rome.

"I just wish I could speak your language better," Tiro said.

Don said, "The way you speak doesn't matter too much. It's what you are like that matters."

I asked him what he meant.

"When I chose to follow your God," he said, "it wasn't your words that made me decide. It wasn't even the prayers that God answered – or didn't answer. It was because you were like no one else I'd ever met." He looked at each of us. "I was a stranger, but you took care of me. You didn't reject me because of my sickness. Bryn, you even risked death for my sake. The three of you are closer than brothers, although you all come from different tribes. And so I knew that when you spoke about God's love, it wasn't just words. Your God is real, and you know him."

As he spoke, I thought about Prince Mark. He hadn't believed me when I told him the Romans were coming. But he believed those men who rode back to the fort – for it was plain how scared they were. He realised they had actually seen the Romans. The news was true.

And I realised: it takes more than words to convince people. However much we talk about God's love, people will only believe us if they can see it for themselves. When they see how God's love can change our lives – that's when they'll start to believe it.

***

Before we set out on our journey south, Don was baptised in the river. Half the village came to see this strange ritual. Mother and Enid were there. Not Conan – he said he was too busy mending the thatch on Margaid's roof. (But I saw him watching from his high lookout point.)

As Tiro helped Don out of the water, he said, "May you be the first of many. I pray that one day there will be thousands in this land who trust in God."

That was hard to believe, I thought, looking around. A handful of ordinary people in a small village, part of an unimportant country on the edge of the empire... But God himself often starts things in small ways. And although we may be weak, he is strong.

Our names will never be famous like Queen Boudicca's. No one will sing songs about our heroic life and death. And yet we may be at the forefront of an army – a great army of God's people, outnumbering even the Romans.

Who knows? The Romans may not always rule Britain. In a hundred years, or a thousand, they may be forgotten. But I will pray that the name of God will never be forgotten here, in the land of my birth.